T

UK Dark Series

UKD 2

Chris Harris

COPYRIGHT

CHAPTER ONE

"This is Colonel Moore speaking, who am I talking to?" I started to smile.

"Hello, my name is Tom. Do you happen to have a brother called Jerry?"

"Jerry! How do you know him?"

"This is his radio we're contacting you from. Don't worry, he's fine and living with me. Fiona, Larry and Jack are all OK as well." I paused then added, "Give me ten minutes and I'll get him for you. His story will be better coming from him."

I looked over at Russ, who had the walkie-talkie in his hand. He contacted Pete and explained where we were, and asked if someone could bring Jerry to us as soon as possible.

Colonel Moore's voice boomed from the radio, "Yes, if you could do that, I would appreciate it. Don't take this the wrong way, but I need to verify with him that you are who you say you are. Even talking to you is breaching most of the protocols we have in place." He broke off for a moment or two and then continued, "but we are in unusual times and sometimes protocols need to be altered to fit the current situation. I'll wait for Jerry to contact me."

The radio went silent. I had a feeling that the Colonel had a lot more to say, but I understood the necessity of making sure we were genuine. It was quite possible that Colonel Moore's location also housed what remained of the British Government, and although I had numerous questions I was burning to ask, I realised that for once I would have to be patient.

The next ten minutes felt like the longest of my life until, leaning over the parapet, I noticed Jerry and Allan jogging up to the church. I shouted down and directed them to the entrance to the belfry.

Before long I could make out their laboured breathing as they climbed up the steep spiral staircase. Kneeling down and poking my head through the trap door, I waited until they appeared, both out of breath, in the belfry.

Once they'd climbed the ladder and were standing on the walkway, it took about thirty seconds for them to recover enough to take in what I had to tell them.

Jerry obviously already knew about the radio and the fact that Russ and I had been attempting to make contact, but it was all new to Allan. I gave him a brief explanation as to why we were sitting at the top of a church tower with a military radio. He wanted to ask more questions, but I didn't give him a chance. "Hang on a minute, Allan. Let me just explain to Jerry, and it'll all become clear."

I told Jerry that we had managed to contact his brother, but until Jerry could prove to him that we were genuine, it couldn't go any further.

Jerry smiled at this, but I could see that he was struggling to compose himself and process the fact that his brother had survived.

After a few moments he said, "Typical Jon, he always wanted to be James Bond. I know just what he's going to ask me. We invented a secret language when we were growing up, and we had various code words so that we could tell each other what we were thinking. Come on, show me how to work the radio and I'll speak to him. Just promise me you won't laugh."

Grinning, Russ handed Jerry the handset, saying, "Just speak into the handset, it's ready to go."

"Jon, this is Jerry, can you hear me?" Jerry looked at me, but before I could respond, the radio burst into life.

"Jerry. Before we continue, I need to check that you are OK. Don't worry if you're not, we know where you are and I know there are others listening into our conversation. So this next message is for them. If my brother and his family are being held against their will, or have been harmed in any way, I have a team of highly trained men on standby who can be dispatched at a moment's notice. You will not be able to hide from them."

After a pause to allow us to digest this information, he said, "Jerry, can you remember our code?"

Even though we all knew it wasn't going to be a problem, there was something about the way he'd made the threat that sent a chill down my spine. Everyone looked worried until Jerry broke the mood, saying, "Don't worry about him, he's full of wind. He's always been good at talking big, let me sort this out." Putting the handset to his mouth he replied, "Oday Noj. Am Sweet."

"Yerrj. Probs no."

We looked at each other in amazement and Allan started laughing uncontrollably.

Russ looked at Jerry and said, "Some secret language. My dog could come up with something better!"

Jerry grinned sheepishly and said, "Come on, we were eight at the time." Getting back on the radio he continued, "Jon, can't you come up with another way of checking? It's embarrassing! One of my friends is laughing so much I think he's going to damage something."

When Colonel Moore responded, we could hear muffled laughter in the background and barely suppressed amusement in his voice. "Yes I agree. Do you remember when you broke Cousin Robert's arm when you pushed him off his bike?"

"It was Cousin Roberta's leg you broke," replied Jerry. "You pushed her out of the treehouse, because she'd stolen your favourite Action Man."

Jerry hesitated, then spoke again, "Look, Jon, the people I'm with are good people. I met Tom just before the EMP thing hit and I owe him my life. What we, as a group, have achieved when everything around us has fallen apart, is amazing. I'm not here against my will and I don't know how else I can prove it to you, other than revealing more of your embarrassing secrets to whoever is listening in at your end. Trust me Jon, it's all OK."

"Jerry, shut up! I believe you. It's going to cost me a lot of drinks at the mess to shut people up. But then I suppose as commanding officer, keeping up morale is a priority. Thank God you're OK ..." There was a pause, as if he'd been interrupted. "Jerry, do you know how to make your radio secure?"

Jerry looked at Russ, who nodded, gave the thumbs up signal and pressed a series of buttons on the radio's control panel. He then motioned to Jerry to carry on.

"Jon, can you still hear me?"

After about thirty seconds Colonel Moore replied, "Yes you are confirmed as secure. No other radio can now listen in."

"Why? Who else is out there, Jon?" asked Jerry.

"We're not quite sure at the moment. It's best if we follow a strict security procedure. The information I'm about to give you must not be passed on. Jerry, under normal circumstances I'd be shot for telling you this. Can you trust the people around you?"

Jerry looked us all in the eye and replied, "I trust these people with my family's lives."

There was a minute's pause and we realised that Jerry's brother was debating what to tell us.

"Jerry, please don't interrupt, just let me finish before you ask any questions. As you know, just over nine weeks ago the world experienced an unprecedented disaster. The EMP created by the solar flare was stronger than any model predicted. It was far more powerful than anyone had thought possible, stronger than anything created by nuclear explosions. We can't begin to predict the damage caused. Global communications have failed. Anything electrical that wasn't in a Faraday cage, or protected by something similar, has been damaged beyond repair. Most of the machines and vehicles we believed would be unaffected by the EMPs are inoperable. We can only guess at what's happening in the rest of the world. We've modelled the results on what little information we've received or have been able to gather ourselves.

"The UK Government, in whatever guise you want to call it, be it political or military or police or local authority, has ceased to function." We listened in silence, struggling to absorb what he was saying, as he continued,
"We were all assured by the experts that this would never happen. But as it turns out, those experts were being advised by the manufacturers that whatever they were making would be proof against EMPs. Unfortunately, we believed them and that left us completely unprepared."

He explained that he had been left in charge of a massive army base, probably the only one in the country still capable of operating at anything approaching normal capacity. He was only in charge because not one of the higher ranking officers had arrived. Most of the people in authority hadn't turned up, because the reports they'd been given had downplayed the severity of the situation.

Protocols had meant that certain key government people and other prominent figures had arrived, and some military units had relocated to the base. But that was it.

Contact with other government facilities around the country had been patchy. Most had, or were about to, run out of supplies. There simply wasn't enough food in the country to feed everyone. The initial humanitarian effort had worked, but it had soon become clear that without further supplies, which were never going to arrive, they were only delaying the inevitable.

In the past they had stockpiled everything. There had been warehouses full of food and clothes and anything else that might be needed. But with all the cutbacks, everything had either been sold off or had operated on a "just in time" system from the suppliers. There had been no reserves to fall back on, and more importantly, even if they'd had the reserves, there was no way of distributing them. There just weren't enough working vehicles to make a difference.

In the days preceding the event, he had just been following orders, had assumed that everyone would be doing the same, and had been too busy to notice if they were anyway. It was only after the event that they had sat down and realised what a total mess it all was.

"Jerry, I could go on forever, blaming everybody. The fact is, it doesn't matter who's responsible, it's just too late. We're in this situation now and looking for people to blame would be a waste of effort. The world will have to adjust, change and rebuild. We'll probably need a whole new way of life."

CHAPTER TWO

It took us a minute or two to realise that Jon had stopped talking. We were all absorbing what we had just been told. Yes, we had probably known it anyway. We'd had no contact with anyone in authority, apart from the local police, since it had happened, so everything Jon had told us made sense. Yet having it confirmed still came as a shock.

"Jerry, are you there?" The radio broke through our thoughts as Jerry lifted the handset and replied,

"Yes, sorry Jon. We're still here. Just trying to take in what you've said. I think we all realised that things were bad, but we always hoped that help might turn up some day. You said key government personnel are with you. Surely other people would have turned up by now? Even if they're walking or at least travelling by bike, others should have reached you?"

"Jerry, until I've cleared it with the individuals involved, I'm not going to mention any names. There is a reason why nobody else has turned up. Nobody knows where we are. The location I'm speaking from has been one of the best kept military secrets since the Cold War. I'm not even sure why it still exists. I was on the roster to be the staff duty officer, to be transported to the base in the event that the base went on alert. I've been on the roster before. The only thing you are told is that in the unlikely event of the base being activated, you will be contacted and instructions will be given.

You're picked up from a preselected place and taken to the base. If you're not at your pick up point at your appointed time, you don't get here. I can only assume that's what happened. Most people just didn't take it seriously and missed their lift."

The idea of secret government bases and military secrets all sounded a bit far-fetched, but here we were talking to someone on the radio about it. Frustrated, I asked Jerry if I could speak to his brother.

He handed the handset over.

"Hello Colonel Moore, it's Tom again. I'm glad you're all OK and sitting nice and safe in your 'lair' BUT, please don't take this the wrong way, do you have any idea how many people have died out in the real world in the last few months? I understand everything you're saying about the lack of supplies, and I'm not sure what you could have done to help, but surely you could have tried something!"

Even as I was saying it, I was beginning to understand the impossible position they had found themselves in. Food can't be produced out of thin air. Vehicles for transporting food can't be repaired if there are no spare parts. I spoke again, "I'm sorry, my brain hasn't caught up with my mouth yet. I'm sure you would have helped if you could. Just ignore me."

Colonel Moore came back on the radio, "Thank you Tom. Believe me, if we could have made a difference we would have. But whatever we could have done would only have scratched the surface, and then we'd have been in the same situation as everyone else. It was the hardest decision any of us has had to make. We 'battened down the hatches' and sat it out. God forgive us for making that terrible choice. But we knew that with the resources and equipment we have available to us here, at some point in the future, we could help to make a difference, and start building a new world out of the chaos we are facing as a result of this disaster."

Over the next hour, we all took it in turns to relay details of our story to Jon. He'd quickly told us to stop addressing him by his rank. For one thing, we were civilians, and didn't need to, and for another, we had saved his brother's life and therefore he considered us friends.

By now we were receiving repeated calls from Pete over the walkie-talkie, desperate to know what was going on, so Allan and I elected to go back and leave Jerry and Russ talking over the radio. We asked Pete to send two armed volunteers to the church, to act as guards for the two of them, and to escort them back when they had finished.

Walking back to the road, we passed the two volunteers walking up to the church. They were desperate to know what was going on, and said that everyone knew something momentous was happening and had all stopped work and were just hanging around, waiting for news.

We decided to wait for Russ and Jerry to return before getting everyone together for a meeting, but to have a quiet word with Pete first, just to keep him "in the loop".

As soon as we were through the barricades we were surrounded by people desperate to find out what was going on. We had a hard time telling them to be patient for a little longer.

While Allan distracted the crowd, I indicated for Pete to join me in my house. Becky, Fiona, Jane and Michael were waiting at the kitchen table. I shooed all the children out and shut the door so that we could have some peace and quiet.

I told everyone what had happened. I apologised to Pete for not telling him about the radio, explaining that I hadn't wanted to get anyone's hopes up before we knew it worked. Fiona was the happiest, knowing that her brother in law was OK. Becky looked a little pensive and Jane and Michael, who were still getting used to our community (they had only arrived the day before and had not even begun to recover from their own terrible ordeal), looked decidedly dazed.

I asked Becky what the matter was. "I don't know," she replied, "It's obviously great news that we're not alone after all the pain and suffering we've seen and experienced. I just don't want this to change things. Do these people think they have a right to tell us what to do? We're working hard to get this right, but we stand or fall by our own choices. Do we have to bow to their will or agree to do what they say?"

I looked at Becky in admiration. She was thinking ten stages ahead of me (as usual). "Becky my love, I don't know. Only time will tell, but all I can say is when I was speaking to Jon, I got a feeling that he is one of the good guys. Am I right, Fiona?"

Without any hesitation, Fiona replied, "Yes, he's great. If he's in charge, then we'll have nothing to worry about. He's a really good man."

I asked Fiona to tell us more about him.

He'd been in the military since leaving university. He'd seen active service in all the recent conflicts, and had been decorated for bravery on a number of occasions, climbing steadily through the ranks over the years.

He had never married, and with all the moving around that his job had entailed, had found it hard to maintain a steady relationship. Fiona laughed and admitted that he'd been so good looking in his uniform, he'd driven most of her single friends a little bit crazy. At one stage he'd threatened to stop visiting, because Fiona's blatant matchmaking efforts were making him feel like a horse being put out to stud. She assured us that if we ever got to meet him, we would like him instantly.

Russ and Jerry arrived back with more news. Jon was planning to visit, and once his team had worked out the details, he would let us know when to expect him.

He had also asked one of his signallers to explain to Russ how to rig up an extended antenna for the radio, to save us having to climb the church bell tower, and how to perform basic maintenance on it to keep it functional. Jerry suggested that we all work on a wish list of equipment or supplies that we wanted or needed, as Jon had promised to do his best to help.

We then went outside to inform the crowd, and to put them out of their misery. Everybody was over the moon and the clapping and cheering went on for a long time. Pete, once he had calmed everyone down, passed the meeting over to Jerry, Russ and me so that we could answer any questions. After the third question about food and supplies, I had to interrupt Jerry and say,

"Friends. This is not it. We have not been saved. Yes, we have made contact and are shortly expecting a visit from Jerry's brother, Colonel Moore. But we still have to work hard to survive. We can't expect these people to feed us or do our heavy work for us. They're in the same position as us. Yes, they may be able to help us, but I'd also like to think that we can help them. We've all survived and we can pass on what we've learned. The future is looking brighter. I believe we are emerging from the dark and a new dawn is coming."

CHAPTER THREE

Over the next couple of days, Jerry and his brother were in regular contact. Jon admitted that the "little trip" he had envisioned was rapidly turning into a major expedition, as more and more personnel and government figures were finding compelling and well-argued reasons as to why they should be included.

An unmanned aerial vehicle (UAV) had been launched, and the route mapped and planned to avoid any major obstructions. Jon admitted that he had so many "gadgets and gizmos" at his disposal, and people with plenty of time on their hands, that even though it seemed excessive, planning this mission had galvanised a lot of his people back into action, and made them aware that they still had a job to do: rebuild the country.

The wish list we'd put together comprised mainly spares and parts that Russ wanted for his various projects.

Allan had requested weapons, to help improve our already quite impressive security arrangements, and more razor wire, as he wanted to extend the security perimeter. We hadn't had a positive response about the request for weapons, but it hadn't been ruled out either.

All I'd requested was a cockerel.

We couldn't get a definite answer on how many people to expect. It appeared that Jon didn't know himself, and was desperately trying to keep the numbers low, and therefore manageable. (We got the impression that he was failing).

Although Jon assured us that they wouldn't be encroaching upon our hospitality and would manage their own accommodation and supplies, we decided it wouldn't be pleasant to sleep under canvas in December, so Pete set about preparing more houses in the road to accept guests. Not knowing how many to expect, we "aired and prepared" the ten houses that were directly next to the block of ten we all lived in.

Allan erected a basic security fence around the properties, removed the fences separating the rear gardens, and cut down trees and shrubs to improve visibility.

We fully expected Jon to arrive with a strong military force, so we were not too worried about security, as we figured they would be able to manage that themselves. But what Allan had accomplished would give them a start.

Rumours were flying around about who was expected to visit. Jon refused to be drawn into any conversations about it, and changed the subject every time the question arose. This did nothing to stop the rumour mill; it only made it worse.

Pete had to resort to losing his temper to get most people back on track. A holiday mood had settled over all of us, and he was finding it difficult to get everyone motivated to do the daily tasks he set for them. One good rant from Pete, using some well chosen and considered words, embarrassed us all back into compliance.

The one allowance he did make was a request for more baking supplies from the kitchen crew. They were determined to go on a "bakeathon" and show off their cooking skills on the new and improved "Beast". Russ had continued to tinker with it and nowadays it barely leaked any smoke. He'd also added controls to regulate the air flow, which helped to control the temperature.

Over the weeks the volunteer cooks had learned to tame The Beast. The quality of the food was improving, and recipes were being adapted or invented to suit the supplies that were available and the sheer number of people there was to feed.

We were all losing weight. With all the extra physical work we were undertaking, and the more controlled portions we were receiving, (and the lack of snacking opportunities), all of the adults were getting into shape. The women were calling it the "Disaster Diet" and the standing joke was that it should have been invented years ago.

It would have saved them all a lot of money and time wasted on following the latest exercise or diet crazes.

Jerry was monitoring us all closely to ensure that we were staying healthy. He was actually carefully documenting his results, and treating it as a research project to show how regular exercise and a controlled diet improved general health over an extended period.

Common sense really, but as he explained, it wasn't often you had the opportunity to conduct a study like this over such a long period of time on such a number of people. He was hoping to prove that common ailments such as asthma could be helped, or even eradicated, by following our enforced healthier lifestyle. His initial results were looking promising. We were all feeling fitter and healthier, so we were not surprised.

Jon had expressed amazement when we told him what Jerry was doing.

All he would say was that a few of the people who might be accompanying him on his expedition would want to sit down and discuss various matters with us.

When we next spoke to Jon later that evening, he announced that all the plans had been finalised, and they would be leaving the base at midnight, and aiming to arrive at our location by mid-morning tomorrow. Christmas Day.

Although I wasn't on guard duty, I found it impossible to sleep that night, so I crept quietly out of bed so as not to disturb Becky, and grabbed my MP5. I walked over to the barricade, where I knew Allan was on guard duty.

He quite often volunteered for the worst night shifts. His argument was that most of the others had family here. He also insisted that he didn't mind pulling "the graveyard shift" as it gave him some peace and quiet to plan his next security project. In reality, I knew it was because he was just being thoughtful and felt guilty when others were doing the unenjoyable cold and dark shifts.

I found him sheltering in one of the lookout posts he had constructed along the barricades, to protect the sentries from the worst of the weather. I handed him one of the insulated mugs of coffee I had brought with me and he moved over to make room for me to sit down. I told Jim, the other man on duty, that I'd take over his watch for him. He didn't take much persuading, because the night was cold, with a biting wind. He shouted his thanks over his shoulder as he rushed home to his wife and his warm bed.

We passed the time chatting about various subjects. Russ was working on some sort of lighting to improve night time security, and we chuckled as we pictured him apologising for the crudity of his design, and unveiling something that would far exceed anything we could possibly hope to invent.

We had started calling him Scotty (the engineer from the original Star Trek Series) and our dreadful attempts at a Scottish accent saying, "Och the energisers are crossed like a Christmas tree cap'n it canna take nee moore!" amused us far more than it did him.

Allan described various changes he wanted to make to our defences and we talked them through. Usually when we discussed something, we ended up with an improved idea.

I could tell Allan wanted to discuss something else and was feeling awkward about it, so I took a wild guess and steered the conversation towards Michelle. He immediately opened up. We had become close friends over the weeks and I was pleased that he trusted me enough to talk about it, and in the dead of night there was also no risk of anyone overhearing. He clearly needed to get it off his chest.

He had fallen madly in love with Michelle, but didn't know what to do about it. I was touched by the emotion in his voice when he talked about his feelings for her. Even I had enough emotional intelligence to realise that now was not the time for silly comments; this was a serious "man to man" conversation.

His anguish stemmed from the fact that he didn't know how Michelle felt about him. He'd tried being a friend to her, to help her through the trauma she'd suffered, and now he was afraid that she thought of him only as a friend, a big brother figure, and that he'd ruined any chance of love.

I put my hand on his shoulder and said, "Mate, look, I may not be the most sensitive person when it comes to understanding women's emotions, but every time you walk into my house, Michelle's eyes light up. You're included in most of the conversations she joins in with. She's always asking one of us if you're OK, and she paces up and down looking worried when she knows you're out on patrol. Now if that's not love, then I don't know what is! Look," I added, "if you want me to have a quiet word with Becky, who by the way loves nothing more than a bit of matchmaking, I'll be more than happy to do it."

"Cheers, mate," he said, looking relieved."Appreciate it." At this point I couldn't resist winding him up a bit by adding,

"Of course! I've worked it out. Jerry's hunky 'James Bond' brother's arriving in a few hours isn't he? He'll be wearing a better uniform than you. No wonder you're worried!"

His response made us both laugh, and with that, our conversation went back to normal topics.

The rest of the night passed in pleasant conversation between two good friends. When the next shift arrived, we all shook hands and wished each other a Merry Christmas. Allan and I walked to our respective homes. I invited him back to my house to share Christmas morning with everyone in the house. He thanked me and said he'd be over in a while, once he'd spent some time with the people in Pete's house. He told me he had some Christmas presents he wanted to give to Michelle.

CHAPTER FOUR

Despite the children knowing that Christmas was going to be radically different this year, the magic and excitement was still enough for them to wake up early. We'd warned them that Santa wasn't going to be able to deliver as many presents this year, but they were still as excited as only children can be on Christmas morning.

In the last few weeks the scavenging parties had been carrying a wish list of items that parents thought their children would like (and a more secretive list for wives, husbands and partners).

Most requests had been ticked off the list. By universal agreement, no gifts had been scavenged from houses that contained dead people. It seemed acceptable to take things from houses that people had abandoned, but to make a gift of something that had belonged to someone who had died, just seemed wrong.

As a community, we had all agreed on the format for the day. Each household would exchange gifts and spend a little family time together before congregating in the communal cooking area. A day's holiday had been declared and only the barricades would be manned. The shifts would be rotated every hour to give everyone a chance to join in the planned festivities.

It was all the more exciting because of the impending arrival of Jerry's brother and an unknown number of extras.

We had thought about inviting some of the more friendly groups of survivors we had come across to join us for Christmas. We'd even discussed it with some of them on joint scavenging trips. We had all agreed that it would be a good idea to arrange a get together at some point in the future, perhaps more of a conference than a celebration. But as we were by far the largest, best organised and best armed group in the local area, there was a risk that we might look as if we were showing off about how much better off we were.

Most of the groups were barely surviving, and living in squalid conditions. In the end we decided against it.

We had always tried to offer help and advice to these people, but we couldn't afford to offer them anything more than that. More often than not, we had given them more than their fair share of the scavenged food. Despite this, some groups were looking in worse condition every time we met.

Perhaps selfishly, we also didn't want anything to ruin the day for our children.

The kitchen in our house was packed, as every resident of the house gathered together. All sixteen of us!

The children received their presents first. After some hasty organising the day before, Jane and Michael now had presents to give to their children.

I gave Stanley his first knife; it had a fixed blade and a leather sheath. I gave him the usual lecture about what would happen if I thought he couldn't be trusted with it.

Daisy got a nice painting set. Bless them! They were both over the moon with their gifts and never once looked disappointed about only receiving one thing.

Most of the presents the adults exchanged related to keeping warm. I gave Becky a nice fur hat I had found and she gave me some good quality leather gloves. Everybody else exchanged hats, scarves, socks or gloves.

As we all stood or sat around in the kitchen, it struck me that it could have been a normal scene from any family Christmas. Even the log burner I had installed in the old fireplace didn't seem out of place. The only thing that struck a jarring note was the gun rack I had built for the shotguns and my MP5, to keep them safely out of the way and to stop people tripping over them.

If an outsider had lookcd at thc people in the room, they would have noted that our clothes weren't as clean as they had been, or as well pressed.

We probably looked dishevelled and a little grubbier than before, as washing was now regarded as a luxury that used precious hot water.

But the things that the outsider would have thought normal were the genuine smiles and laughter that filled the room. Kids were running around excitedly and parents were having to raise their voices to make themselves heard over the increasing noise level.

Allan arrived with the presents for Michelle. She'd talked to him a lot about the things she had been most upset about losing and subsequently, he'd been to her house to look for them. The house had been ransacked and a lot of the items of sentimental value had been smashed, damaged or stolen, but he'd managed to recover some treasured photographs and some of her favourite pieces of pottery, which he'd painstakingly glued back together.

She looked at him in shock when she realised what he was giving her.

This quickly turned to a look of panic, and she burst out crying and ran upstairs.

Allan looked crestfallen. As he turned to leave Becky said, "Where do you think you're going?"

"I've upset her and I didn't mean to. I'll just leave and let her be alone, I don't want to make it any worse," he replied with the best "lost puppy" face I'd ever seen on anyone.

To his astonishment Becky just laughed, "When are you two ever going to realise that you love each other? It's so obvious to the rest of us. She's just realised that you may love her, but is afraid to find out that you don't, so she's run away. You think you've upset her and she doesn't love you, so you're about to run away as well! If you don't get up those stairs RIGHT NOW and tell her how you feel, I'll ban you from ever stepping foot in this house again!"

The poor man absorbed what Becky was telling him and transformed from a lost puppy into the happiest man in the world. He took one look at me, smiled and ran up the stairs, calling her name.

I interrupted the cheers and whistles from the happy crowd of onlookers and said with a big smile, "Shall we go outside and meet up with everyone else? I'm not sure I want to explain to the children the noises we might be hearing from upstairs soon." We all agreed, laughing, gathered up the children and pointed them in the direction of the door. The women seemed to be in some sort of race to be first out, presumably so that they could be first to reveal the latest gossip to the other occupants of the road. The happy news about Michelle and Allan was received with universal pleasure and raised everyone's spirits all the more.

The planning that had gone into the Christmas meal was impressive, and after a breakfast of porridge and cereals, various people were tasked with childcare and supervision duties, while others were allocated food preparation duties.

Precious fresh vegetables had been scavenged and hoarded, and geese, ducks and even swans had been shot and prepared for cooking.

The quantity prepared had been increased over the last day or so, in spite of Jon's insistence that we were not to use any of our supplies to feed our visitors. We had decided that it would be rude not to offer them some hospitality, especially when they were arriving on Christmas Day.

Extra camping ovens and barbecues were brought in to prepare the feast and soon the delicious smells drifting over from the kitchen had us all drooling at the thought of what was to come.

The next hour or so flew by with everyone in a good mood. Yes, tears were shed when missing loved ones were thought of and talked about, but we all knew we were lucky to be alive and were thankful that the community we had formed was surviving against all the odds.

We couldn't dwell upon the ones we didn't know about. The joy of reaching a landmark date like Christmas Day alive, was an achievement that we all wanted to celebrate. And the impending arrival added to the excitement of the proceedings.

The people who still wore watches glanced at them frequently, wondering when our visitors would arrive.

At about eleven o'clock, the distant noise of diesel engines silenced us all, and as a group, we all started to move past the barricade and walk up to the line of cars blocking the top of the road.

CHAPTER FIVE

We all stood and waited.

Two armoured vehicles appeared suddenly, coming up the main road from the direction of Kings Heath (the next "village" along, about a mile further out from the city centre). I didn't know what the vehicles were called but I had seen them on television. They'd been used for transporting troops around Afghanistan. They had huge machine guns on top, manned by soldiers.

As the vehicles slowly approached, we all stood there quietly. Jerry, Pete and I walked forward a few paces into the middle of the road and waited for them to arrive. I was glad that the guns in the turrets were pointing to the side, the vehicles were intimidating enough without having them pointed at us.

The lead vehicle stopped and a soldier in full kit climbed out and made his way towards us. "Hello there. Which one of you is Jerry?" he asked.

Jerry said, "I am."

The soldier took a photograph out of a pouch on his body armour and held it up, comparing Jerry to it. He was quiet for a minute as he studied us all individually, and then he looked at our families and friends, standing a few yards behind us.

"Well I'd say you were all genuine!" he said finally, extending his hand and shaking ours. "Sorry about that. We've been monitoring you via UAV since the initial contact, but I'm the first 'eyes on the ground' we've had. I had to confirm that Jerry isn't being held under duress." Unclipping his radio handset from his body armour he said, "Would you excuse me for a moment?"

As he Turned away, we heard him say, "No, confirm Jerry situation good."

Grinning, he turned back, "We just had to use your code words, they were so 'special'. Now if you don't mind, my men need to do a quick security sweep of the area before the main convoy arrives."

He waved at the soldier at the front of the lead vehicle. In response the rear doors opened on both vehicles and sixteen heavily armed soldiers stepped out.

"Don't worry, this won't take long. It's just standard procedure. The UAVs haven't picked up anything in the local area apart from the locations of the other groups you've given us, (they'd requested this information during a previous radio conversation as part of their route surveillance).

He apologised for not introducing himself properly, "Captain Wales, Commander of the expedition's lead element."

A few minutes later a soldier approached and told him that the area was clear. "Good. Maintain a perimeter until the rest arrive. But monitor the UAV operator's channel closely." Reaching into another pocket, he pulled out a bag of tea bags, smiled and said, "I don't know about my men, but I'm desperate for a cup of tea. I couldn't borrow some hot water could I? I've got some milk and sugar in the back of the vehicle if you want some."

There was something familiar about the Captain, but I couldn't put my finger on it. Laughing, I replied, "No, we're fine for milk and sugar. Come down to our kitchen area. I'm sure we can spare you some water."

"How long will the rest take to arrive?" Pete asked.

"Oh, about thirty minutes, I would guess. We regrouped at the motorway junction and it'll probably take them that long to get moving again?"

"How many of you are there?" I asked, still trying to place where I knew him from.

"We're a complete circus. If Colonel Moore hadn't overridden a lot of requests, it would have been worse! We are one hundred and fifty soldiers plus support staff and twenty civvies. Just under two hundred of us, I believe."

A look of horror must have passed over our faces. "Oh, don't you worry about it," said Captain Wales, "We're very self-sufficient. We'll try not to get in your way too much."

"It's not that," replied Pete. "The ladies have been baking cakes and are now cooking a Christmas dinner we were hoping to share with you. I just don't think we have enough to go around. They're going to be mortified!"

Lowering his voice Captain Wales said, "I believe we're planning something similar. So shall we keep the numbers to ourselves until they turn up? We wouldn't want the lovely ladies to get all in a tizzy, would we?"

I agreed and turning to everyone, I suggested we head back to the communal area, as the others wouldn't be arriving for at least another half an hour.

It took a bit of persuasion to tear the children (and some of the grown up children) away from the excitement of admiring the armoured vehicles and soldiers.

The Captain walked back to the barricades with us, escorted by two of his men. As we were walking, he removed his helmet. Then it hit me. It was Prince Harry!

"You're…you're … him!" I stammered.

"Yes, sorry," he said, looking a little embarrassed. "It's a bit awkward I know, but I'm better at the soldier stuff than the royal stuff, so I volunteered to lead the mission."

We were all shocked. I didn't really know what to say next. It wasn't often you met and got to chat with a member of the Royal Family. And here we were, about to offer him a cup of tea and a slice of homemade cake! The only way I could think to deal with it, was to carry on as normal.

I shook his hand again, "What do we call you? You're a lot more used to this than we are. If you could give us an etiquette briefing I think it would save a few embarrassing moments for everyone."

With a straight face, he replied, "Your Royal Highness would be the correct way to address me, followed by a short bow." At the looks on our faccs hc laughed and said, "I'm sorry, it gets me every time I do it. I do apologise. Call me Captain or just simply Harry, or if that's too much for you call me Sir, but I'd much prefer Captain or Harry."

Taking an instant liking to him, I decided to go for broke. "Harry, could I offer you a seat and a cup of tea?'"

Handing the tea bags over to me, he said, "Yes, but could you possibly see that my men get a mug first. I'd really appreciate it."

He went up another few notches on my respect rating. I spotted Allan and Michelle, who were walking over to us arm in arm, and gave them a big smile. They'd missed all the excitement of the arrival and looked a bit lost in each other.

Allan didn't notice Prince Harry sitting on a bench in full kit until he was right in front of him. He spluttered, let go of Michelle's arm, and tried to tidy up his uniform with one hand and give a salute with his other, while coming to attention and saying, "SIR!"

Michelle almost fell over when she realised who he was saluting.

"Thank you, Constable," said Harry, smiling, "but please relax, I'm just an Army Captain."

Standing up, he shook Allan's hand and said, "You must be PC Harris. Thank you for not forgetting your duty, and for trying to serve these people, when most people had given up and were only looking out for themselves. You're a credit to your uniform and to the Government, who, I'm sure, will want to acknowledge your service at some point in the future."

Allan went bright red, turned to Michelle and said, "Sir, may I introduce Michelle, my fiancée, to you."

At the mention of the word fiancée, we all forgot about the presence of the Prince, and the cheering and clapping spread as the news was quickly passed around. Everyone rushed forward to congratulate the happy couple. The women all burst into tears and the men immediately started talking about the stag do.

Harry came up to me and said, "A recent decision I take it?"

"Yes. They only managed to get together an hour or so ago, despite everybody else knowing they were in love. They were the only ones that didn't. But being engaged, that's taken us all by surprise."

"What you've all managed to accomplish here, from what I have been told and what I have seen in the short time I've been here, is nothing short of a miracle," said Harry, seriously. "I believe you're mainly to thank for this, Tom. People are so happy that they are getting married and planning a future. Do you know how powerful and important that is?"

"I wouldn't say that, Sir." (I don't know why, but it seemed appropriate to call him "Sir" when we were talking business).

"All I did was work out beforehand that it was going to happen. Yes, I'd prepared for something like this, so I did have food and equipment stored away, but without all the other people joining in, we wouldn't have survived. We wouldn't have made it past the first attack. Everyone's played an important part in this group's survival. I'm absolutely over the moon about Allan and Michelle and now you've said it, I can see it's another landmark we've achieved." I paused for a moment, thinking.

"Tom, I think we all know that's not true, but I admire your modesty. I think you'll have an important role in helping this country get back on its feet."

I couldn't help adding, "You mean *your* country Sir. You're the Royal Family!"

Laughing, he replied, "No it's not mine, its Grandmama's really!"

Changing the subject away from me, I asked him why a leading member of the royal family would be "out in the line of fire".

"I'm hardly a leading member anymore. My brother keeps producing babies! But now I'm further down the royal chain, I get a bit more freedom. William can have the job, he'll be far better at it than me. And since there are currently no royal engagements in my diary, I thought the least I could do was help out and do what I've been trained to do. I did pull a few strings to get on this expedition, but I may as well get some use out of my name."

"How many Royals are at your 'Secret Base'?" I asked.

"Oh not many. I'm not really sure what I'm allowed to say, because I wasn't paying attention at that part of the briefing. Let's wait for the main element to arrive and I'm sure all will be revealed."

I knew he was stalling, but realised that it wasn't worth pushing it. As he'd said, all would be revealed shortly.

Understanding everyone's curiosity and noticing that most people were just staring at him or pointing him out to their children, he turned and said to everyone,

"Hello all. Yes it's me! We're all going to be very busy, as in a short while, as you know, a lot more visitors will be arriving. We're going to be here for a few days, so I'll get the chance to introduce myself to all of you, but I will need to get my men settled in and equipment set up. If I could just have some time to do my job, I would appreciate it."

A message must have come through on his radio, because he held his hand up to his earpiece and listened for a moment. He replied, looked up at Pete and me and said, "They're going to be here in about five minutes, shall we make our way to the top of the road?"

I nodded and Pete told everybody to start heading in that direction.

CHAPTER SIX

As we waited at the top of the road, we heard the distant sound of lots of engines. It seemed an alien sound after the enforced silence of the past couple of months. I couldn't help wondering how many people would hear the noise and come to investigate.

We hadn't had a chance to inform the other groups in the area about what was happening. We would need to go and see them soon. In the meantime, if certain undesirable individuals or groups decided to pay us a visit, aside from our own highly effective security force, we now had the might of the British Army protecting us.

The first armoured vehicle came into view. Then the convoy appeared. There were many more armoured vehicles, trucks, and articulated lorries, and a number of vehicles I couldn't identify, but which looked extremely impressive. Most trucks were towing trailers or bowsers, presumably containing fuel or water.

The convoy looked huge and stretched far away into the distance.

Turning to Prince Harry, I said, "There's got to be more than two hundred people here."

"I know it looks that way, but we have a lot of equipment to use and we weren't sure what we would need, so we decided to bring a bit of everything. Probably overkill, but this is the army and there's no such thing as too much kit. We had it and we had to bring it. We probably all got carried away because, for once, there was no one to remind us about budgets and costs. Boys and their toys and all that!"

I just laughed and shook my head at the ever growing procession of vehicles coming in to view.

By now the lead vehicles had reached us. Harry spoke into his radio to remind his men to keep their eyes pointing outwards for any potential threat.

Silence descended over the road, as one by one, the vehicles stopped and shut off their engines.

The silence was palpable. In the city, we'd been used to the constant noises that bombarded us every day. After the event, the silence had seemed strange and had taken time to get used to. Now the noise of all those vehicles sounded just as alien, and the silence when the engines went quiet felt normal, better.

People started to step out from the vehicles.

"Jon!" shouted Jerry. To the amusement of those around him he ran forward and threw his arms around his brother. Once he had disentangled himself from his brother's embrace, Colonel Moore walked over, hugged Fiona, Larry and Jack, and asked to be introduced to the rest of us.

I was tempted to carry on the hugging tradition, but decided on a hand shake instead.

The introductions were a blur: Captain this, Lieutenant that. It was fortunate that they were all wearing name tags because I had no idea how to tell the ranks from their lapel badges or shoulder thingies.

I knew I'd have to learn quickly or I might start upsetting people.

"Right," said Jon briskly, "first things first. Peter, Allan and Tom, we need to discuss security. Everyone needs to be clear on what they're doing. We can't afford any confusion or unfortunate mishaps, so I suggest a quick planning meeting between my lot and yours. Bring anyone along you feel is relevant. We'll let our people mingle for a while, but please keep an eye on the young ones. I'd hate them to touch something they shouldn't and get hurt."

We adjourned to Pete's house where his dining room had been turned into his office. On the wall were large-scale maps of the area with key points marked on them. There was also a well drafted drawing of our current set-up on the road, with all the occupied houses marked, (including details of all the occupants), and showing the locations of all our defensive points.

The visitors admired them before we got down to business. We began by explaining our current procedure.

We'd already provided details during our previous radio conversations, so most had heard it all before, but for clarity we ran through it all again. Our scavenging procedures were also discussed. Although we all knew the men and women who would be coming and going, a soldier on guard duty wouldn't know if the armed people heading towards him (or her) were friendly or not.

One or two of the officers started to tell us what we should or shouldn't be doing, and what was acceptable. Before any of us could react, Jon interrupted them and apologised, saying,

"Please, gents. We're the guests here. This is not a base, where what we say goes. Our procedures will have to fit around theirs, not the other way round. Like it or not, I think we can learn a lot from these people. They've all survived without the benefits of warehouses full of kit, and have adapted well to the situation we are all in. No matter what you think," he continued, seriously, "I doubt if any of us could have done a better job."

To be fair, they all conceded the point and apologised and the meeting continued. Initially it was agreed that a soldier would accompany every individual who was on guard or patrol duty. We hadn't planned any scavenging trips for a day or two, so we decided to discuss that later.

We told them that we'd prepared some houses just outside the perimeter for them to use and had put basic security measures in place. They were overjoyed about this, and confessed that no matter what way you looked at it, sleeping under canvas in winter was something to be endured if necessary, and avoided if at all possible.

One of the officers went to check out the houses and quickly returned to confirm that they were ideal. With a few more cots in each room everybody could easily be accommodatcd.

They planned to set up a security perimeter around their vehicles, which would meet with our perimeter at the barricade of cars.

They would assume the responsibility for patrolling that perimeter, and the barricade would be opened to allow easier access between the two. We agreed that at least initially, anyone entering the road where the vehicles were parked should be accompanied by a uniformed member of the expedition. That way they could easily be identified as legitimate and not some outsider sneaking in.

It all made sense, but I was conscious that there were a lot of people outside, including my own family, who all had a right to be involved.

And it was Christmas Day.

"Gentleman and ladies," I interrupted everyone, "could I request that we adjourn this discussion? Unless anyone thinks differently, I believe we've covered all the important stuff for now. Some of us have been busy cooking you all a welcome meal, and I don't have to remind you it is Christmas Day, and the only duties we have today are guard duty. So whoever is in charge of allocating duties to your personnel, have a chat with Pete here and get it sorted. I'm going to spend the rest of the day with my family and friends, and I'm including all our new arrivals, when I say friends."

Colonel Moore stood and smiled, "Well said, Tom. Our cooks have been planning something similar, so let's go outside and meet everyone else. Can I suggest we all try and restrain ourselves and leave all the questions we have until tomorrow? As Tom rightly says, it is Christmas Day and I don't think Santa has been here properly yet."

The atmosphere on the road was great. The sun was out and temperatures were mild for the time of year. Everyone seemed to be getting on well, and the road was noisy with the sound of people chatting and laughing. Colonel Moore and Pete went to sort out the guard routine, prior to briefing the residents and soldiers who were due to be on guard duty. In the meantime, Allan and Harry updated the rest of the road's occupants on the plans we had made.

The plans had been hastily drawn up and would need improving, but given what we already had in place and the fact that Jon's engineers were already quickly surrounding their perimeter with coils of razor wire, I told myself I could afford to relax.

Jon (as he had virtually ordered me to call him) confirmed that their base would continue to provide UAV coverage and would provide advanced warning of anybody approaching.

I was desperate to ask more questions about the "secret base" and had to keep telling myself to be patient, something I wasn't very good at.

At the kitchen area, the army chefs and our cooks were deep in conversation, intermingled with the odd burst of laughter. I spotted Becky and the children happily chatting with others, and wandered over to check that everything was going to plan and to find out if there was anything I could do to help.

They were all in good spirits and I realised why, when I noticed a bottle or two being handed around and glasses being filled. Joining them, I was soon handed a glass filled with whisky, which I tried to decline as I was due on guard duty later in the afternoon and we'd all agreed to limit our alcohol intake until after our shifts.

Those of us who either didn't drink at all, or were happy to abstain, had kindly agreed to take the later guard shifts to allow those of us who enjoyed a tipple the chance to let our hair down. Community spirit in action!

I was quickly filled in on the plans. With what our cooks had prepared and what the army chefs were planning as a surprise, there was more than enough food to go around.

They'd brought one of their mobile kitchen units with them and asked if they could set it up in our kitchen area. The cooking capacity needed to be increased and it made more sense to do all the cooking and preparation in one area, so it could be managed better. I told them I would arrange for a path to be cleared.

Once the kitchen unit was standing next to the Beast, I was very much reminded of Beauty and the Beast, and I hoped that Russ wouldn't be too upset. The army's new and shiny mobile cooking trailer, with its fold-out work tables and gas operated ovens and hobs, looked seriously impressive next to Russ's cobbled together contraption. When I mentioned this all the cooks quickly jumped to the Beast's defence, saying that no matter how nice and shiny the new unit was, there would always be a place in their hearts, and their kitchen, for the Beast.

It was announced that Christmas Dinner would be served at approximately half past three, but if anyone needed a snack before then, the kitchen, thanks mainly to the army chefs, would be offering a continual stream of pasties and sandwiches.

The main gossip was that Anna, the self-styled boss of our kitchen, and the head army chef, a sergeant who looked as if he'd done a lot of boxing in his time, had had a little turf war over control of the kitchen. Anna had won outright and the sergeant was now treating her with so much respect and admiration, it was comical to watch.

The sound of a gunshot stunned us all for a single moment.

CHAPTER SEVEN

Allan shouting, "Everybody into position now!" got everybody moving. As the soldiers grabbed their weapons and looked round for orders, our community moved quickly and decisively. Children were grabbed or pushed in the direction of my house. The men and women whose emergency positions were at the defences, quickly ran to fetch their weapons and moved to their pre-determined positions.

Within two minutes everyone was in position and Pete's radio received the call that everyone was accounted for in the safe house (mine) and that it was locked down.

The soldiers were all still on their radios asking for reports and looked as if they weren't receiving any. Allan ran up shouting, "Lower barricade!" He indicated for me and a few others to join him and we raced down to the wall at the bottom of the road. I saw Prince Harry give a signal and then follow us with a group of soldiers.

At the wall of tonne sacks, there was already a line of our people and one soldier crouching down low and looking over the wall. Those with weapons were pointing those outwards, towards whatever threat was out there.

Allan looked confused about who should be in charge, as he was standing next to Prince Harry. Realising this, Harry quickly said, "You're Head of Security. This is your wall. I'm following your orders."

Allan nodded, "What happened, Dave?" he asked the man who was on duty at the wall.

"Not sure, Allan," he replied, "I was just standing here with Gary," he gestured towards the soldier next to him, "and the next thing, we both saw some movement further down the road, just past the line of cars. I was looking through my binoculars when BANG! a bullet smacks into the shelter, just missing my head!" He pointed to the splintered hole in the side of the wooden shelter next to him. "Since then, nothing!"

Harry spoke up, "I've Just received confirmation that the UAV isn't overhead. It's developed a fault and returned to base, and they haven't got the next one ready for launch. Colonel Moore'll rip somebody's head off for this. We need coverage."

"Well, we've got by without it so far!" said Allan. "Let's do this the old fashioned way."

Still crouching behind the barricade, he cupped his hands around his mouth and shouted, "Why did you fire on us? We've done nothing to hurt you."

"We followed your soldier buddies here," said a voice. "We're not going to allow some false government to take control of our area. Surrender now and you'll be allowed to join us."

We all looked at each other in amazement. "What are they on?" I whispered. If it wasn't for the fact that it was happening, it would have been funny. "I haven't got a clue what they're talking about. What area? Who do they think they are?"

Harry replied quietly, "We've been picking up rumours about some idiots setting themselves up as warlords in a few places. Food is power, so if they have control over a warehouse or distribution centre, they can control the locals, using food as leverage. As he said, they must have followed us here."

"Then why haven't you done anything about them yet?" asked Allan.

Harry shrugged. "We haven't confirmed they actually exist yet," he replied with a wry smile. "We've discussed various scenarios, but the problem is, there'll obviously be a lot of innocent civilians involved, who are only there because of the desperate situation they're in. We haven't come up with an alternative, other than if we come up against one, we'll have to go in 'all guns blazing'."

"Shall we call this confirmation then?" replied Allan, "What on earth do they expect to be able to achieve against us? Especially now that you're here!"

"It's difficult to say. Maybe they just want to test us. See if we'll give them something to go away. Or they may actually think they're military geniuses who are capable of outsmarting us, and leading a successful attack against a heavily fortified and well trained force who are expecting them. Stranger things have happened. Let me try and speak to them."

He shouted over the barricade, "This is Captain Smith. What do you want?"

I looked at him, "Captain Smith?"

He shrugged, "It's better that saying, 'Hello, Prince Harry here!' I don't think that would help the situation. Do you?"

Colonel Moore arrived at this point with a few other officers and a couple of soldiers who were obviously his security detail. "Damned annoying, this. How rude of these fellows to come and ruin our fun, what!"

He was clearly trying to calm our nerves by playing the stereotypical British Army Officer, stiff upper lip and all that.

Harry joined in, adding, "Couldn't agree more, Sir. Permission to leave and return to the rear, where I was just finishing my tea and chatting to some rather lovely ladies."

"Permission denied, Captain Wales. For the sake of the harmony of the group, I've already received a number of requests to keep you away from all civilian wives and girlfriends. Your harem's already full!"

The bantering served its purpose. Everyone visibly relaxed and there were a few audible chuckles. Job done. Back to business.

Harry looked at Allan, who nodded to him to proceed. He quickly filled Colonel Moore in on what had been happening and the details of our brief conversation.

"Okay. Rules of engagement. They opened fire without warning, therefore I consider them extremely hostile. No negotiation. We'll eliminate the threat."

Looking at Allan and me, he asked, "I know this is your patch, so to speak, but I think it would be better if we took it from here. It's what we're trained for after all."

We both nodded in agreement.

The same voice shouted back, "We'll let you stay here for now, but you'll have to pay a tax in food and weapons. We need as much food as we can carry and twenty of the soldiers' guns."

Colonel Moore snorted. "These have got to be the dumbest, most moronic idiots that ever roamed the Earth. Captain Wales, play along like a good chap and ask them how many there are so that we can 'sort out the food'. And ask how much ammunition they'd like. Remind them that it's heavy duty stuff."

Harry shouted his reply.

While we waited for an answer, someone commented that they were probably busy removing their shoes to help them count if they ran out of fingers.

Colonel Moore turned and introduced Allan and me to another of his soldiers. He'd been at the briefing earlier but had been silent throughout. "Chaps, this is Captain Berry. He's ….er our ……," he thought for a moment.

"Oh, bugger it, no time for cloak and dagger stuff. He leads our special forces detachment, so I'm sure you know what regiment he belongs to."

We both shook his hand. He was a normal looking bloke, not the muscle-bound superhero type we'd have expected but he had an air of supreme confidence, and after exchanging a few words, we could tell that he would be a good person to have on your side and was certainly not someone you'd want to cross!

The enemy's response had finally come back, "We need food in twenty five rucksacks and another five rucksacks full of ammunition. You have thirty minutes to get it ready. Don't try any funny business or you'll regret it!"

By now most of us were sniggering. "Okay, Einstein out there has now reliably informed us that there are most likely thirty of them," said Colonel Moore briskly.

"That probably means only ten of them are armed, and they're running out of food, because they've prioritised that over ammunition. If you hadn't already worked that out, that is." he added.

A few more soldiers had arrived and they were keeping out of sight behind the barricades. One was carrying a heavy looking machine gun and another a few boxes of ammunition. After a quick conversation Colonel Moore turned to us and said, "To put your minds at ease, we've dispersed our machine gun squads to reinforce most of your positions. All our soldiers are on full alert and one of our armoured vehicles is ready to move out if necessary. Don't worry, nothing will get through us."

I had no doubt about that.

Captain Berry walked up to Allan and me, asked for a moment of our time and we followed him back to the kitchen area. To my astonishment the army chefs, now decked out in body armour and helmets and with their weapons slung on their backs, were still busy cooking.

Captain Berry saw our expressions and said in a voice loud enough for them to hear, "Oh, we don't want dinner ruined. They'll have to carry on. And they're all such lousy shots anyway, they'd have more chance of killing them with food poisoning than with their weapons."

The cooks flung a few good natured comments back at him, along with a few rude gestures, and cheerfully carried on with their work.

Getting a tablet computer out, he asked us to look over his shoulder. The screen was showing an aerial shot of the road. The clarity of the shot was amazing, with every detail picked out. When he zoomed in, I could even see an overhead shot of myself on it.

"I remember wearing that sweater a few days ago." I said. 'We didn't even know it was up there! The picture quality's unbelievable."

Captain Berry, or Paul (as he'd asked us to call him) grinned and replied, "Well it wouldn't be much good as a spy camera if you knew it was there, would it?"

He rotated the map.

"It's like Google maps on steroids," I said. He changed the angle to give us a full 3-D view of the road.

"Where do you think the technology came from?" he said. "What you can do with overhead shots on your home computer is nothing to what can be done with military technology. It's just that we don't want everybody to be able to do it. Now, could you show me where you think the shot came from?"

I pointed to the line of cars further down the road and he quickly changed the view on the screen. "With your knowledge, what's the best way to get there unseen?" he asked. He was back in professional mode and the mood was more serious. I suggested a route to him which would involve going over or through a few back garden hedges or fences. He plotted the route into the computer and the view changed to a simulated walk through the proposed route.

The technology was impressive, but not infallible. I pointed out a few places where the computer had interpreted what it was seeing wrongly, and with a few strokes and swipes the necessary changes were made. Technology like this was clearly a huge advantage on this kind of planning mission. From a series of overhead photos, a complete walkthrough of the mission could be simulated.

He thanked us and immediately called his men, who were gathered close by. He ran through the mission with them and showed them the planned route. At Paul's request, Allan and I stayed, in case any questions arose that he might not be able to answer.

A couple of minutes later he stood up and announced his intention of clearing the mission with Colonel Moore before proceeding.

He was back a minute later. "It's all go," he said. Then pointing at me he carried on, "Tom, you'll need to come with us. Time is of the essence and if we encounter a problem, your knowledge of the area could save lives. There's no time to discuss this. We'll need to be in position well before the thirty minutes are up. If you could go with my sergeant here, he'll kit you out."

Five minutes later I was wearing a full black tactical vest festooned with magazines, grenades, radios, the lot. The radio was set so that it was on continuously. All you had to do was speak into the mic and everyone could hear you. I was told not to touch any of the grenades. I was just carrying them in case the others needed more.

My position in the line was second from the rear and I was told in no uncertain terms that if anything happened, even though I was carrying my MP5, I was not to do anything unless my life was in danger. They were the experts.

I was so excited I forgot to be scared. I was living every boy's dream (large or small!). I was taking part in an SAS mission. I hadn't even had time to talk to Becky. She was still in our house, together with the rest of the community that weren't involved in defence.

On the signal, Harry, who was still at the barricade, started shouting questions to the attackers, ludicrous questions about food preferences or whether they would prefer tins or packets.

It was truly ridiculous, but listening over the radio, we could tell that it was having an effect. The enemy were quarrelling among themselves about what they wanted.

Shaking his head, Captain Berry summed it up, "Honestly, if they're that thick, they deserve to die. We'll be doing the gene pool a favour!"

Our trip through the gardens was uneventful and in no time at all we were in position. We were now a few houses further down the road from where the line of cars had been constructed as our first line of defence.

One of the soldiers was sent ahead to investigate and we watched as he crawled forward, using every available scrap of cover to hide his approach. He reported that the head count was twenty eight and it was clear to approach, as the enemy were all crouching behind the cars, facing towards our barricade.

I was told to remain and watch the rear, so I faced the other way with my gun at the ready, as the others crawled forward. Soon, over the radio, I heard all the members of the team reporting that they were in position and ready.

Next came the order, "Leave the one with the red cap on. Neutralise the rest in 3-2-1 now."

I heard the sound of suppressed gun fire in repeated bursts. I could only image the carnage caused by eight superbly trained men opening fire at close range on thirty or so unsuspecting victims.

One by one the reports came through over the radio, "No more targets, area clear."

I was trying to be a good soldier and resist the urge to turn and watch, when a sudden noise to my right made me swing round. Two men were emerging from the doorway of a house between me and the soldiers. One of them was carrying a shotgun and was in the process of aiming it at the soldiers, who hadn't heard or noticed them. I didn't know what they'd been doing, but they had to be members of the gang, and one of them was about to shoot at the exposed backs of Captain Berry's men.

Without thinking, I raised my weapon, pointed it at them and pulled the trigger. At some point I must have switched my weapon to full auto, because when I pulled the trigger it spewed bullets in the direction of the two men. In a matter of seconds the gun clicked empty and the two men lay in a heap in the bullet-splintered and pockmarked doorway of the house.

I stood there, slightly shocked, but pumped full of adrenaline.

The sound of a soldier's voice beside me made me jump, "Cheers, mate, good one! Now if you'll keep watching our rear, I'll go and check those two and see if there are any more surprises." As he and another soldier ran off, he turned and added, "Might be a good idea to reload as well."

Feeling like the rookie I was, I ejected the magazine and loaded a new one, while I watched the two men check the bodies and make sure that there weren't any more of them that we didn't know about.

Watching the rear, I jumped again a few minutes later when Paul tapped me on the shoulder. "All clear. Great job. You saved us there. It was my fault, we knew there should be thirty of them and when Private Anderson counted twenty eight of them, I didn't make the connection. Bit embarrassing really."

I spluttered a bit as I tried to think of something to say. Looking around, the bodies of our would-be attackers lay where they had been shot.

Soldiers were checking them all for signs of life, removing any weapons they had and piling them in one area. The one in the red cap, who had been allowed to live, was lying on the floor with his hands tied behind him, guarded by two soldiers.

It was a scene I'd witnessed before and one I knew I would see again. Dead bodies, lying at the strange angles they were in when death found them. The lives of twenty nine people had been extinguished in a matter of seconds, but I didn't feel the least bit of guilt or sympathy towards them. They'd been trying to harm us and deserved to die.

How things had changed in just a few months.

I could hear cheers and clapping from beyond the barricade. The news of our success had obviously spread. "Shall we get back?" asked Paul, 'The bodies can't be seen from the compound, so we'll deal with them later. We have other priorities at the moment." He nodded up the road.

CHAPTER EIGHT

As we walked back through the gate at the south barricade, we were surrounded by well-wishers all wanting to congratulate us. Looking over their heads I saw Becky, Stanley and Daisy running towards me. The "all clear" had obviously been given and the occupants of the safe house had been allowed out. Pushing through the crowd, I gave them all a hug. Becky broke away from my embrace, took one look at me and said, "What are you wearing?"

I was still in the Special Forces body armour and helmet. The vest was still festooned with grenades, and magazines for my MP5 were stuffed into every pouch.

"I……er……um……was sort of asked to go as a guide," I replied somewhat sheepishly.

Becky's voice changed to her "You are in SO much trouble" voice. "WHY YOU? Do you have to volunteer for everything? You could have been killed! What would have happened then?"

I was saved from more of this by the arrival of Colonel Moore and Prince Harry, who took pains to thank me for helping out and congratulated me on ensuring the success of the mission. Becky, unsure about whether it was acceptable to berate your husband, while he was being congratulated by a member of the Royal Family, opted for stony silence.

I looked gratefully at Harry, who gave me a wink and a "you owe me one" look.

Colonel Moore turned to address everyone, "Sorry about the interruption. But I know we'll all be keen to get back to where we were before. The need for vigilance and protection has just been demonstrated. My engineers will soon have the extra fences finished, and Pete and I have worked on the guard rotas. So please rest assured that with our help, you'll be as safe as houses. Aerial surveillance is now back up and running, after its untimely failure, so we'll have advanced warning of any more unwanted visitors."

Questions were asked by a few people, as they had been unaware of the UAVs flying overhead and most people seemed reassured by the fact that there were others watching out for us. I wasn't sure we should relax too soon though, as we'd only just beaten off another attack.

I could tell that Becky hadn't had the final word and I was desperate to avoid it, so I told her that I needed to return the body armour to Paul. I felt a bit dangerous standing there with all those grenades hanging off me. She chose to accompany me, so we all walked up to the now open barricade of cars and waited for a soldier to escort us to where Paul and his men were.

As we came round an armoured car, we were met with the sight of his bare backside, just before he pulled on some underwear. His men noticed me, Becky, Stanley and Daisy behind his back and started to laugh. Spinning round and realising he was being stared at by Becky and my two kids, he quickly grabbed a sweater and tracksuit trousers and pulled them on.

"Sorry, just changing out of my kit," he said, looking mortified.

"Great," I thought, *"Not only is he an SAS captain, he looks a bit like James Bond, he's got a posh accent, so his parents probably own half of Warwickshire, and he's got a six pack as well! What's not to like about him?"*

I introduced him. He gave Stanley and Daisy a salute and shook Becky's hand. Becky didn't seem to want to let go of his hand and she had a bit of a glint in her eye.

"Becky, put the nice SAS Captain down, please," I told her, laughing.

"OOH, but look at him. He's gorgeous," she replied. He looked a bit uncomfortable at this point. "I'll just look at him for a bit longer if you don't mind." Then her voice changed, "Because if he ever takes my husband on a stupid gung ho mission again without asking my permission, I'll personally make sure he's not so pretty anymore!"

With that she smiled sweetly, came over to me and put her arm around me. His men burst out laughing. I just stood there, then decided to join in. Paul looked a little taken aback, then realising Becky had got the better of him he grinned, saluted her and promised never to upset her again.

Reluctantly I handed the kit back to Paul and he removed the grenades. When he saw how wistful I was looking, he handed it back to me saying that after what I'd done today I deserved it. I received it with glee. Although Allan and I weren't generally competitive, I knew he'd been seething with jealousy when he saw how much better my kit was!

At this, Paul seized the opportunity to praise me to Becky and began to tell her about how I'd saved some of them from getting shot today. Seeing the look on Becky's face, I hastily interrupted, saying, "I think that's enough about that for now. We don't want to be upsetting my lovely wife now, do we?"

Paul asked us to wait while he went off to get changed, so that he could accompany us back to the main compound. A few of his men asked where we'd put the prisoner and I explained that Allan had probably locked him in the police cells. I pointed across the road in the direction of the police station and saw Allan and a few soldiers heading back from there.

I waved at him to get his attention and he walked over to us. He confirmed that the prisoner had been locked in a cell with a toilet bucket and some supplies and they planned to question him the following morning. He hadn't revealed much yet apart from the fact that they were based near Redditch (a town just south of Birmingham), and used bikes to get around when they were out scavenging.

He was just off to find Jon and Pete, and discuss whether it was worth sending out a patrol to find the bikes.

Becky gave him a hug and congratulated him once again on getting together with Michelle.

Embarrassed, he walked off to find Jon and Pete, and once Paul had joined us we set off.

The road sang with the sounds of joy, laughter and happy conversation. We now had plenty of hands to help and with some rejigging, the plans to seat and feed over two hundred and fifty people were progressing nicely.

The kitchen was a hive of activity, with Anna, backed up by her loyal Sergeant, orchestrating all the men and women who had been roped in to help.

In spite of the unfortunate interruption, we were still on track for a half past three Christmas dinner. In the meantime Pete continued to coordinate the guard shifts so that they changed regularly and no one missed out on the fun.

A small group of soldiers appeared with what looked like portable lights and began to set them up. Spotting Harry, I asked what they were up to.

'We've brought this bloody great generator with us and the engineers have rigged it up so that we've got power for heating the temporary accommodation you've given us. The generator's got plenty of capacity, so I've given them permission to set up lighting in the street. I thought it would cheer the place up.' He paused for a moment. "I'm sorry if it was a bit presumptuous, but I thought it would be a nice surprise."

"How could we be upset by street lighting? We've only just got running water back to the road."

"Oh I think there's a lot we can help you with in the short term. But let's leave all that till tomorrow shall we?"

Pete came up to me with a concerned look on his face. "What's the matter?" I asked. Harry turned to leave, but Pete said, "I think we may have an issue and it does concern you, so if you could stay please?"

"What's troubling you Pete?" asked Harry.

Pete shuffled his feet and looked uncomfortable. "We've just realised we've got swan on the menu. Yes, we have eaten it before, but we're aware of the law that says only Royals and Fellows of a Cambridge College are allowed to eat swan and now we have a Royal present, people are worried."

Amused, I looked at Harry, and was impressed by his ability to keep his face straight. Harry looked serious for a second, avoiding my eye, and replied, "I tell you what, when I get back from this little trip, I promise I'll get an amendment or extension or whatever the law calls it, and get the residents of this road royal permission to eat swan. In fact, I'll perform a Royal Duty and announce it at the dinner."

"Well, thank you, Sir," said Pete, looking relieved. "I'll go back and tell them not to worry about it. But I won't tell them what you're going to do."

I started to laugh and Harry looked sideways at me and grinned, "Thank you for doing that," I said, "I've just had a thought, with that little proclamation, you've probably just added a whole chunk of money to the value of our houses. Shame money doesn't matter anymore!"

As we walked over to join the others, we had a silly conversation about how future estate agents would fall over themselves to include the swan eating law in their sales literature.

The dinner was a resounding success and as everyone had a couple of quick stints on guard duty between courses, no one missed out on the opportunity to have some or all of their Christmas dinner with their family and friends. Prince Harry's announcement that Royal permission was to be given for everyone in the road to eat swans was greeted by wild cheering and applause.

Once the dinner was over, and before washing up duties began, Jon stood up and gained everyone's attention by banging two metal cups together.

"It wouldn't be Christmas without a visit from Father Christmas. So I had a word with the man himself and he's decided to pay us a visit!"

A man (well you couldn't quite tell but it must have been one of his subordinates) walked into view dressed in a not bad cobbled together Father Christmas outfit, complete with a large sack slung over his shoulder.

Jon continued, "Would all the children form an orderly queue please? I'm pretty sure he has something for everyone."

I'm not sure if the resulting melee could quite be described as an orderly queue, but eventually order was restored. Soon all the children were excitedly tearing open presents that kept appearing from the sack.

Jon walked up to me and in a loud whisper explained, "One of the supply vehicles that was diverted to our location contained a pallet of toys. This seemed like a nice way of distributing them." We were overwhelmed with gratitude.

Once all the children were happily sharing or playing with their new toys, Jon got our attention again. "Now, Christmas is not normally just about giving children presents. I apologise to the grownups, as Father Christmas clearly didn't receive all your letters, but he did bring presents for a few of you."

He waved his arm and a few soldiers appeared, carrying some boxes. One box was perforated with holes and he opened this one first and reached inside. He lifted out a very irate looking cockerel. "Now who asked for this chap?" he asked.

I shouted, "Me!" and smiling, I went up to Jon to collect my gift. Just before I got there the cockerel set about Jon and made a successful bid for freedom. Chaos ensued as residents and hardened, battle trained soldiers alike, attempted to pounce on McQueen (as the cockerel became known), then ran from his vicious attacks each time he was cornered.

By the time he was captured most people were helpless with laughter. Still squawking in outrage, he was taken to the chicken run and immediately perched himself on the highest point and announced his arrival by continually crowing at the top of his voice.

After ten long minutes of crowing, a number of people were reminding me that they were armed and threatening that if my bird kept them awake or woke them up early, he might well meet with an unfortunate accident.

All I could say was, "Keep thinking about fresh roast chicken, and forgive him."

After everyone had calmed down, Russ was presented with a large container which, he was assured, contained most of the spares or parts he was missing for his next invention. Jerry and Fiona were each given a small box of medical and dental supplies, as requested, with the promise of more to come.

Finally Jon informed everyone that his Quartermaster had brought a lot of sundry supplies with him and that he would be "opening up shop" tomorrow.

If anyone wanted to see if he had anything they needed, they were welcome to come and have a look.

The cheers and applause he received when he sat down continued for some time.

After we'd all quietened down, Paul, the SAS Captain, stood up and spoke, "As a regiment we don't often give out awards. The things we do aren't really talked about. But today something happened that deserves a mention."

At this point I felt myself going red and Becky nudged me. A few of the others looked over at me and started to smile. "Today," he continued, "someone stood up and faced odds that were stacked against them. They ignored the danger and triumphed over adversity."

I looked up at this. Surely this is going a bit far? I thought.

"Ladies and gentlemen. I would like to present the Beret and title of 'Honorary Member of our Regiment' to someone who stood up against an entire platoon of us, defeated us all and won our hearts. …' he paused and I started laughing, as it was now Becky's turn to blush. "To Becky!"

The cheers, catcalls and applause for Becky lasted even longer, as she was presented with her Beret and a pair of underpants (clean!) signed by all of them.

The rest of the day passed amidst great companionship and shared laughter. At dusk, when the lights were turned on, nobody wanted the evening to end. Everybody wrapped up warmly and stood around the braziers (scavenged oil barrels with holes punched in them) that had been lit, enjoying the warmth radiating from the burning wood, and the friendships, old and new, which were being cemented by the occasion.

Eventually the evening began to wind down, as people became conscious that they were up for guard duty in the morning, or would have other responsibilities to see to. Most people decided to turn in for the night.

Allan and Michelle came up to me. I hadn't had a chance to congratulate them privately about their new status as a couple, as they'd been surrounded by well-wishers for most of the day. I seized my opportunity, gave Michelle a hug and shook Allan's hand again.

They told me that Michelle was going to be moving to Pete's house to be with Allan, as our house was very full and we didn't have an available room for them. She was feeling bad about leaving after we'd been so kind to her. I told her not to worry. Yes, we were going to miss her, but she was only moving over the road, so it wasn't as if we were never going to see her again. Besides, I added, she and Allan would probably need more privacy than our house could offer them.

With that, I gathered up Becky and the children and wished everyone good night. I was due on the early morning guard shift and was feeling exhausted after the day's excitement. A few neighbours and soldiers were still sitting around chatting and drinking and it looked as if a bit of a session was starting.

The soldiers must have been given permission, because Jon, their commanding officer, was present and didn't look too worried about it. The neighbours were responsible for their own actions, so if they woke up with sore heads in the morning, it would be their problem.

Becky noticed me looking over at them, sighed and said, "Go on then. Get me and the kids to bed and you can go and join them."

Boy, did I have a thick head in the morning!

CHAPTER NINE

The next morning the serious business began. After a huge breakfast of pastries and bacon sandwiches, courtesy of the army chefs, Jon asked for permission to address us all as a group. As there were no objections, his soldiers replaced our guards on the barricades and we all gathered in the kitchen area to hear what he had to say.

"Friends," he began, "I'd like to start by thanking you all for the welcome you gave us yesterday. It shows what a good group of people you all are. I know what you've all accomplished together and it's nothing short of a miracle. The fact that you've also tried to offer help to others is also quite extraordinary. On behalf of the Government, I applaud you." At this point, he and his officers and advisers stood up and clapped us (much to our embarrassment!).

"Considering everything you've been through, you've all earned the right to know what's been happening to our country. I'd also like to talk about the recovery plans we've come up with, and gauge your reaction to them. A bit like having a focus group, I suppose."

Some of us smiled at this, but I had a feeling we weren't going to like some of the ideas. Still, as he'd just said, they wanted feedback. I only hoped they'd be willing to listen to us if they didn't like our answers.

Jon continued, "You all know why this has happened, so I won't go into that. The country is now in a desperate situation. There simply isn't enough food for everyone, and we don't have the ability to produce enough without modern farming methods. As you can imagine, these just aren't possible anymore since the event, so we have no way of producing enough food to feed us in the future. Nor can we expect help from anywhere else. Every country on the planet has been affected, and the few we have been able to contact, are all in the same boat."

We sat in silence and he paused for a moment, then carried on speaking. "The Government has always had certain protocols in place to cover every possible crisis scenario, and I'm sure it won't come as a surprise if I tell you that someone, in a small government office somewhere, wrote a paper on what to do if we were ever hit by a global Solar Storm Event. The title of this paper is 'UK Dark'.

"When I read it, I don't mind admitting that I was shocked and appalled at the proposals it made. But the more we all discussed it, the more apparent it became that whoever had written the paper, was right. The projections it contained are unbelievable."

He explained that we were currently experiencing what the paper callously referred to as a "population readjustment". Within six months of such an event, the author expected the population to fall to just ten per cent of its pre-event level. In other words, a ninety percent reduction.

He paused to let that sink in. I did a rough calculation. The population of the UK had been approximately sixty million. So in just six months, it was likely that fifty four million people would be dead, with only six million of us left! That put us back to medieval population levels. Truly staggering figures.

He saw us beginning to stir, as we were probably all doing the same calculations, so he continued,

"Yes, the maths is appalling. We took the truly awful decision to follow protocol, lock down the base and protect the occupants. I'll tell you more about our facility later, but let me assure you, as I said over the radio … "he nodded at me and Jerry, "If there'd been another way of handling it, we would have done it. We simply didn't have the resources to make a difference. We needed to protect what the facility contains for the sake of the future."

Looking grim, he added, "A few of us weren't able to handle the choices we had to make and initially, we did have a number of suicides. But eventually everyone realised that we still had a role to play in whatever recovery plan we decided was best."

"As things currently stood," he explained, "realistically the country had only ever had a few days of food available. As soon as the event hit, most people immediately found themselves in trouble, with only one or two days' worth of food left in their cupboards. Once this was consumed," he continued, "the first exodus from the main population centres began. Millions of refugees swarmed into the countryside looking for food, and many areas were completely overwhelmed. The timing of the event couldn't have been worse. The main harvests were in, so unless people knew exactly where to look, there was very little food to be found.

"After only a few days, the Government's initial humanitarian efforts were exhausted and it was unable to provide any help at all. I must emphasise," added Jon, "that no one is to blame and everyone did their best. It would have been logistically impossible to feed so many people even if we'd had the supplies, which we didn't."

In the meantime, he told us, the cities were becoming battlegrounds. The rapidly diminishing supplies were being fought over, and gangs were assuming control, and robbing and murdering at will.

This led to the second wave of refugees fleeing the cities. These were the people who did have food and had been preparing to wait the crisis out, but fled to the supposed safety of the countryside due to fear, or because they'd been robbed.

This second wave encountered the first, thousands of whom were already dying. The newcomers found nothing but starvation, disease and violence.

Some of the models used for prediction have stated that people living in the countryside are more likely to survive an event of this nature, because the local population is lower, and food, either grown or hunted, is more readily available. This would probably have been the case if the countryside hadn't been overwhelmed by the masses from the city.

Minor wars began to break out as country folk, who normally have easier access to firearms, banded together to protect their properties and land. Thousands were killed before the ammunition finally ran out and the farming communities were overrun.

Although it was hoped that the more isolated rural communities might have escaped the worst of the crisis, Britain isn't a big country so it was possible that nowhere had escaped.

"The Military did try to help," Jon explained. "As you know, we set up refugee camps, but these were inundated and found it impossible to cope. There were also mass desertions, with many of the soldiers leaving to try to help their own families. The collapse was total. We believe one of the last camps to remain open was the one that your sister and brother in law were in, Tom. And that disintegrated over two weeks ago."

Looking at each of us in turn, he carried on, "It's winter, there are millions of people without food and shelter, all struggling to survive in the most appalling conditions. People are facing violence and death on a daily basis. Millions are already dead and unfortunately, over the next few months, millions more will also die. And there is nothing we can do to prevent it.

Our only hope is people like you. People who, against all the odds, have survived, and with skill and determination, have built something special. There must be others like you out there. People who have formed similar communities, and would be willing to help. Yes, there are still people out there, as we discovered yesterday, who would rather resort to violence and intimidation, but they will no longer be tolerated. There are no courts and we don't have the resources to put them on trial and therefore …" he paused, "Martial Law has been declared."

An audible gasp went round the room and people began to ask questions.

In response, he held up his hands, "NO! It's not what you think. The military is not taking over. We still have a sovereign and a government. Good people, such as yourselves, have nothing to fear. You all have an essential role to play in our plans to rebuild the country. It's in our interest to help to protect you if we can.

That said, if we do encounter anyone who's still intent on causing suffering and pain, there'll be no jury or trial. We just don't have the time. If anyone fights us, they will be destroyed."

Holding his hands up again to ask for quiet, he continued,

"I study history and I can guess what some of you are thinking. I know we won't always get it right. Mistakes will be made. If we come across a group like yours, who have no harmful intentions, but choose not to trust us or don't want to get involved, they'll be left alone. That will be their choice. We have no intention of forcing our will on anyone who doesn't want to be involved.

That said, we are hoping to prove to them that they would be better off working with us. Contact would be maintained, but no help offered. If they want to be left alone, they will be. But they'll get no practical help from us.

We have a basic ideology for our country. Some are calling it the first written constitution. The three main principles are:

1.   If you want to contribute and help to rebuild our country, you'll receive whatever help our resources are able to offer.

2.   If you want to be left alone, that's fine. But you'll receive no help in any form. If you want to be on your own, you will be *completely* alone.

3.   If you fight against the system, either by direct opposition to us, or against any community or individual that is helping and contributing to our cause, you will be wiped out.

On the basis of these three simple rules, we hope the country will be able to rebuild itself.

UK Dark predicted everything that has happened so far and has set out basic guidelines to assist us all in the future. It states that six months after the event, once the majority of people have succumbed to disease and starvation, the most capable and resourceful ones will be left.

The 'bad apples' will have been weeded out, but through the somewhat heartless process of natural selection. The people remaining will be exactly the kind of people needed to start over again."

He spread his arms and indicated to all of us standing in front of him.

"To every one of you now, and without irony, I say, 'your country needs you'."

Pausing, he held up his hand to quieten us down. "Let me tell you about the facility, and what it contains. The base, as I've said before, is probably one of the Government's best kept secrets. I'd never heard of it before, not even a rumour, until the day I received my orders.

It's located in Herefordshire, but it doesn't appear on any map. It's disguised as a huge farm and actually operates as one, both arable and livestock. As a matter of fact it's always made a nice profit for the Ministry of Defence.

But hidden on the farm, in cleverly designed outbuildings, underground bunkers and even an old converted mine system, is a vast network of store rooms, office blocks, living accommodation and everything required to sustain a large population for a long period of time. A true product of the vast overspend on the arms race," he added wryly.

The base was, he explained, designed to be resistant to all forms of attack, be it nuclear, chemical or whatever. Its defences were subtle and cleverly designed. The whole base had only a few points of entry and the perimeter, through an ingenious combination of ditches, hedges and fences, was well hidden from prying eyes. It was very difficult to gain access.

"The farmer acts as an outstanding, if slightly eccentric member of the local community and does an excellent job of distracting any attention away from the place, so most recent visitors have been from outside of the area.

We're still following strict protocol, so no one apart from the security patrols, the farmer and a few farm workers are allowed above ground. The perimeter is patrolled by soldiers dressed as farm workers and carrying concealed weapons. The whole base is covered by cameras and sensors, which still work, as they were designed to withstand the effects of an EMP.

The few people who have found us have been picked up by our security details as soon as they've breached the outer perimeter. If they look innocent enough, say they're a family in search of food, they're monitored carefully, but are allowed to get close to the main buildings, where they're met by our friendly farmer and 'interviewed'. If they're local, he gives them some food and sends then on their way.

If they're from outside the area and are genuine refugees, they're offered food in exchange for working on the farm where, after further careful monitoring to corroborate their stories, a decision is made by a panel of randomly selected base residents about whether to let them into the main facility or send them on their way.

Most have been allowed to join us. Anyone breaching the perimeter with hostile intentions, is eliminated immediately. There are no second chances.

I know it sounds unbelievable. When I first arrived I was astounded by the place. All the other rumours and leaks about cold war bunkers, had all been red herrings. I believe there was one up for sale a few years ago, which was supposedly intended to house four thousand people for up to three months. That was just a badly built decoy designed to 'take the scent away' from where we are.

"The reason it's still in existence, is that it hardly costs anything to maintain. It doesn't have a large maintenance crew and is just locked up, awaiting activation. Also, I don't think anyone wanted to make the decision to close it, and be the person everyone would blame if it was still needed, and they had shut it down on their watch.

It was designed to hold a functioning government in the event of a whole variety of attacks or natural disasters occurring. If the country was invaded, the base's secret location would enable leadership to continue for as long as it remained hidden.

The base now houses key members of the Government, including the leaders of most of the main parties and their families. There are also a few members of the Royal Family, a whole raft of advisors and ministers with their families, and of course, a sizeable detachment of soldiers along with their families. And we're not anywhere near capacity.

"The inclusion of families was important. Everyone on the base has an important role to play and let's face it, you're unlikely to be effective if you're worrying about your loved ones all the time. How could we expect the military to stay and help guard us all, if we hadn't looked after their families?

The one thing UK Dark didn't look into in any depth was how we would function as a very small society, ranging from the eighteen year old wife of a Private from a council estate in Birmingham, to senior members of the Royal Family!" He smiled and added, "A lot of social barriers and expectations are being knocked down and rebuilt.

No matter who you are, the food comes from the base kitchen and is served cafeteria style. There are no executive dining rooms for the elite. If you want food, you queue up to get it. There were a few awkward moments at first but I'm happy to say that everyone adapted and got on with it. They were all sensible enough to realise that we are all in it together and we all have a part to play.

For example, that same eighteen year old happens to be a qualified child minder. She's now caring for quite a few important people's children, and enabling them to carry on with their work."

We were all hooked on his every word. You could have heard a pin drop, as nobody wanted to miss anything he was saying.

"According to the UK Dark scenario, once the population has stabilised, we can start helping the survivors to live in this new world of ours.

Yes, we do have a lot of equipment stored. In fact it seems that every time a new vehicle type or machine was ordered by the military, at least one or two of them found their way into our stores. Unfortunately, we still don't have anywhere near what is required, and even though we do have access to the strategic fuel reserves, until we're able to start refining more, we only have finite resources, which must be husbanded for priority requirements.

Our world has suddenly been thrown back to a time where each family will need to learn how to grow enough food for themselves. Holidays will be a thing of the past. Every day will be a constant battle for survival, where one failed crop could mean the difference between life and death.

Horse power will become the new mode of transport. Motorways will lie unused and abandoned, a waste of valuable farmland. Most people's lives will probably shrink to within a radius of a few miles from where they live. Not by choice, but by necessity.

The initial task we face is education. People will have to be made to understand that no help will arrive. They will have to learn how to survive. We can't hold everybody's hand. We can only offer help and advice initially, and then hope that they will share that knowledge to help others.

The supplies that we and everyone else may have stored, your own included, will only last so long.

If you want to eat in the long term, you will have to grow, hunt or nurture your food. If you want new tools or clothes, you will have to learn how to make them.

OK, there will be years and years' worth of goods, such as hand tools and clothes available, just from scavenging, but eventually they will run out. We'll need to re-learn the skills, so that in time we can begin manufacturing the goods that we require. It may be possible at some point, if we can overcome the obvious power supply issues, to get certain factories up and running again.

But all that is in the future. The immediate problem we face is survival. We need to become as self-sufficient as possible and you all have a big part to play in that. Your community will, I think, become the model for what needs to be done. We all have a lot to learn from each other before we can start rebuilding.

Thank you, and may God bless Great Britain."

For a while there was silence before we realised he'd finished then, as one, we all started to clap and cheer loudly.

It went on for quite some time.

CHAPTER TEN

After the applause had died down, Jon and his officers came and joined us for a while. Still patiently answering all our questions, he told us he wanted to introduce us to a number of government figures he'd brought with him.

Allan, Pete and I followed him over to a small group of men dressed in military issue uniforms. I'd noticed them before and had even spoken to a few of them briefly, thinking at the time that they didn't look like soldiers.

Jon introduced us. They were all high-level government advisors and reported directly to the prime minister. They apologised for their uniforms, explaining that Jon had insisted on everyone on the expedition wearing one, so that no individual would stand out as a target.

For the sake of clarity and to avoid any misunderstanding, they asked us if we would start from the beginning, giving them a tour of the whole place and then answering any questions they might have so that they could gain an understanding of how we functioned. They wanted to see if what we had achieved here, could be used as a model for other communities. They were also hoping that their recovery proposals could be used in our situation. In other words they wanted to create a basic plan that could be followed - a blueprint for survival.

Of course we agreed, so the rest of the day was taken up with showing them around and answering their questions. They were particularly impressed by Russ's inventions and what he had achieved just by using the materials that were closest to hand.

The Beast and the water filtration and delivery system had been Russ's main achievements to date, but he was also working on a lighting system, using solar and wind power to charge batteries.

He was still trying to perfect the batteries, but was confident that he would be able to resolve the few issues he was having and that the entire system would be ready soon.

One of the advisors had a scientific and research and development background, and he and Russ spent the rest of the day huddled in Russ's workshop going over the plans Russ had for various projects. We left them to enjoy their "bromance" and the rest of us continued with the tour.

The following day we planned to take them for a walk around the area, so that they could experience first-hand, what an empty city full of abandoned houses and dead bodies looked and felt like. They were keen to experience a scavenging operation and to understand the difficulties people without enough food were facing on a daily basis. It would also be a good opportunity to introduce them to the other groups of survivors we knew in the local area.

Although the weather was much colder now, with temperatures dropping to more normal levels for late December, the mood on the road was still happy and buoyant. And why not? It seemed to most people that our future was now assured. We had made contact with, and met what remained of our government and they wanted us to work with them to help the survivors. We had the obvious advantage of Jerry's personal connection with his brother, the base commander. Surely this would guarantee us a certain level of help in the future? There was a general feeling of optimism among us, a feeling that we'd "made it".

I talked about this with Pete, Allan and Jon. I was aware that we had years and years of continual hard work ahead of us to ensure our survival, and at the moment we were being guarded not just by our own people, but by members of our armed forces. We had army cooks in the kitchen, helping us to provide a continual supply of hot food. It all seemed very "nice", but perhaps a little false.

We decided not to ruin the mood by reminding everyone about the millions of people out there who, without help, would be facing certain death in the near future. Everyone knew it, but there was no point in dwelling on it. After all, we all had friends and family out there and were powerless to help them. Jon had run through the statistics with us on the predicted death toll. It was the stuff of nightmares, with the severity of the predictions depending on the average daily temperature. The one thing that Jon hadn't previously mentioned was the likely result of a city full of rotting corpses. He explained this to us now and we knew that when the temperatures rose we would be facing a horrendous few months.

At the end of the day, just before dinner, Allan and I were invited to witness the questioning of the prisoner from the day before. Harry accompanied us to the police station.

We weren't sure what to expect when we arrived. Would they be waterboarding him? Would they be torturing him to get him to talk?

When we walked into the room and found him sitting at a desk with a cup of coffee in his hand, I wasn't sure whether to be relieved or disappointed. He looked as if he was having a friendly chat with a mate. Grinning, Harry whispered into my ear,

"We slipped him something. It helps loosen the tongue, and seeing as all the human rights lawyers have disappeared, we thought we'd use it."

We listened in fascination as the skilled interviewer got all the information he needed from the man.

The gang was based near Redditch (a town about ten miles south of Birmingham) and was led by a man called Gumin, a local drug dealer and petty gangster. When the EMP had hit, he'd had the presence of mind to take control of a food distribution warehouse on an industrial estate on the edge of the town.

"He uses food as power," the prisoner explained. "If you want your family to eat, you have to do what he wants. They rule over everyone with a rod of iron. Rapes are common place and if you upset one of them, you and your entire family are beaten or killed. Life is cheap and there are always more people to fill the spaces left."

Gumin had been sending out scavenging parties to expand his territory and eliminate any threats to the little kingdom he was creating. He rarely needed to send more than one of his men out with a scavenging party, because if someone tried to run away or disobeyed an order, their family would be killed. It was a cruel but effective way of ensuring compliance.

He had access to an enormous quantity of drugs, both illegal and prescription, and had forced many people into addiction as another means of keeping control.

As most of the people remaining in Redditch had recently been killed or captured, Gumin was now sending out parties further afield to take control of a larger area and find more supplies and victims.

The interviewer pushed the man further. How had they found our location, and why had they thought that attacking us would be a good idea? The prisoner's answer convinced us that, at the very least, this Gumin guy was a psychopath.

He told us that one of their scouts had come across the convoy when it was regrouping at the motorway junction. He had followed it to our location, returned to the scavenging group and led them here. He had known at the time that it would be stupid to attack us, but according to Gumin's rules you didn't retreat from anybody. If you did, you were branded a coward and immediately put to death along with your entire family. There were always people willing to take your place as one of "the inner circle", with all the benefits that came with it.

According to Gumin, everyone was replaceable. Therefore the prisoner had had no option but to try to take something from us. He would have been killed if he'd returned empty handed, so he'd had nothing to lose.

The interrogator questioned him about their numbers, the weapons they had at their disposal, and what their set-up was like, and slowly a clear picture of appalling conditions and brutality began to emerge. Having heard more than enough, Allan and I left to return to the road. Harry, Jon and Paul accompanied us.

Before I could say anything Jon spoke up, "I know what you're thinking. Most of the men we killed yesterday were probably trying to protect their families. You could even call them innocent victims. But at the time, the only intelligence we had was that they were hostile and they were attacking us. I said this morning that mistakes would be made and I'm not even sure this was a mistake yet. I'll need to sleep on it. But I gave the order to eliminate them and I'll take responsibility for it …"

Allan interrupted him, "Look Jon, there is no right or wrong answer. We were attacked and we fought back and won. The benefit of hindsight doesn't come into it. The right decision was made at the time. The point now is what do we do with the information we've got? In my opinion we need to get rid of this Gumin character and his cronies as soon as possible. Yesterday's deaths are on his hands, not ours."

Jon nodded, looked at Paul and raised an eyebrow. Paul nodded, saluted and replied, "Plan on your desk at 0800 sir!" He bid us all good evening and returned to his men.

CHAPTER ELEVEN

After dinner, and once the children were all tucked up in bed, Jon came by with Pete and a few of his officers and advisors, so that we could go over the plans for the following day. His intention was to meet with all the other groups during our tour and, if he considered them to be suitable, to offer them places at the base.

Given the lack of working farm machinery, muscle power, both animal and human, was going to be essential if we were going to work the land in order to start growing enough to feed everyone. In return for their skills and their labour, Jon was going to offer them food and shelter, and he was keen to know what we thought of the proposal.

Our reactions were negative to begin with. Surely this would be no better than forced labour? A prison camp! It would mean going back to a medieval feudal system! But on the other hand, what other option was there?

As long as people were given a clear idea of the future and what was at stake, perhaps they would understand that what they were being offered was fair. What more could people ask for, but the chance of survival?

Finally Michael, my brother in law, spoke up. It was the first time he had joined in any conversation. The horror of the past few months had weighed heavily on him, and he'd admitted in a quiet moment with me that the sheer helplessness he'd felt when he'd been unable to protect and feed his family would stay with him forever. He'd been overwhelmed by relief and gratitude when they'd arrived at the compound, knowing that they'd made it through their ordeal.

"I think I'm probably the best qualified to answer, Jon," he said. "Before this thing happened, I'd have been one of the first to protest that what you're proposing would be slave labour. But now, well, we've tried to survive out there. I've seen friends killed for the contents of their rucksacks. With my very limited knowledge of foraging and survival, I've tried and failed to feed my family with what I could find. And that was before winter had set in."

Tears began to roll down his cheeks and my sister quickly put her hand on his shoulder.

"I'd have sacrificed my own life in a heartbeat if it had meant that my wife and children would live. I've witnessed the evil that's out there. If people don't jump at the offer you're making … if they don't see that this is their chance of finding security, and protection and an opportunity to survive, don't take them in. They don't deserve the chance. If they start to ask questions about how much work they're expected to do, don't take them in. If it meant that my family had a chance to live, I don't care how hard I'd have to work, I'd do it. I'd work my fingers to the bone, knowing they'd have food on the table. Maybe later on, if it still seems unfair, that might be the time to raise concerns. But not now. Not when the offer is first made."

He took a deep breath, struggling for control, and continued, "I've been out there. I've held my children when they've cried themselves to sleep with hunger. You haven't. If people don't jump at the chance, then trust me, they don't deserve it."

Wiping his eyes, he fell silent again. By this time most of the people present had a lump in their throats and Jane, crying herself, gave him a huge hug.

After we'd composed ourselves, Jon spoke up, "Thank you Michael. I can't begin to imagine what you went through. I think you're absolutely right. We need people, but most importantly, we need the right people. I'm not so naïve as to think that only the good will survive, but I truly believe that most people will have the right attitude, the will to …" He stopped and held his hands up, "Sorry I was off again on my 'good over evil speech' but that's not necessary now. I'm glad we all seem to agree on the basic principles. When they're discussed around a table of experts and advisors, it's easy to convince ourselves that we know everything."

Looking around he continued, "We hope our ideas are common sense. It seems the only way to get through this; applying a heavy dose of sound judgement to all ideas and hoping that everyone will see that what we're offering to do, is the right way to go about this.

I'm not sure if Tom has told you yet, but Captain Berry is going to present me with a plan for eliminating this Gumin character in the morning. I've had an idea that I want to put to you. After Paul's briefed me, and if I approve his plan, I'll ask him to set it out for you. I don't want your opinion on the military aspects, it's the humanitarian point of view I'm interested in. No disrespect to Captain Berry. He's as highly trained as they get in terms of hostage rescue and planning tactics. But this situation is unique.

Most of the people at this place will probably have committed atrocities to save their own and their children's lives. So do we regard them as victims or targets? I can't decide. I'm not looking to pass on responsibility, the final decision will still be mine, but I'm prepared to consider other, non-military, points of view. Hopefully it might help me make the correct choice, when I have to."

Having agreed with Jon's suggestion, Pete chose himself, Jane, as she'd had first-hand experience of trying to survive out there, and three other people, selected at random, to join the meeting.

We moved on to the logistics for the following day. Initially we would take a walk around the area, introducing our guests to the other groups that we knew were reasonably close by. We would be accompanied by some vehicles, to provide protection and a fast escape route for the VIP guests if necessary, and because they wanted to give every group some supplies, and the vehicles would be needed to transport these.

The walk would give everyone a chance to experience the empty city.

Once the walk was over, we planned to use the vehicles in order to try to reach the groups that were further away. We hadn't met many of these yet, but our scavenging radius had continued to expand as we'd gradually stripped out anything of use from every house we'd searched. We'd encountered similar groups to ourselves, most of whom had proved friendly, but as our bases had been too far apart, we hadn't been able to ask them to join us on scavenging missions, as we had done with the groups that were closer by. Instead, we'd agreed on rough limits to areas to avoid falling out over territory and the supplies that were available.

Pete and I had planned to keep up some sort of contact with these more distant groups, but as we'd only met some of them once before, we hadn't built up enough trust to be told their locations. Jon wasn't too concerned about this. If we weren't able to locate them initially, he would set up a few UAVs to search for them.

We'd encountered a number of hostile groups too, and up until now had given them a wide berth. It was agreed that we would avoid scheduling any visits to them for the time being, and concentrate on building up a level of trust with the more amenable groups, who were likely to be more receptive to the idea of a recovery plan and life on the base in Herefordshire.

The more unfriendly groups would be contacted at a later date. Everyone would be offered the chance to join in with the recovery plan. But it would be up to them if they wanted to, or not.

CHAPTER TWELVE

Everyone was up early in the morning and the crowd that was gathering in the kitchen area was buzzing with excitement. We were all conscious that important events were taking place today. We were going to reach out and offer help to the other groups we knew of in the area. And if Captain Berry's plans were approved by Colonel Moore, we might also be engaging in our first offensive operations against a vicious enemy.

Captain Berry had chosen not to join us, as he hadn't quite finalized his plan for the attack on Gumin, and he wanted to get it finished for our return. But he was sending most of his men to act as close security for the VIPs.

It had already been agreed that Allan and I would lead the expedition, as we both knew the area and the groups we were going to meet.

Jon and his entourage (soldiers and government officials) would follow our directions, but at the first sign of any danger, control would immediately transfer to Jon, who would lead the military response.

Allan and I had both pointed out several times how nervous people might be at the first sight of heavily armed soldiers. If anything did go wrong, or someone reacted aggressively, then unless people's lives were actually being threatened, the soldiers needed to use careful judgement and not overreact.

Our group consisted of Allan, me and ten of the regular scavengers, who knew the people in the groups we were going to meet as well as any of us. Jon would be joining us, along with all the government advisors, and Captain Berry's men would be acting as their close bodyguards. Prince Harry and thirty soldiers were also coming as extra security. A lorry and one of the armoured vehicles, complete with a machine gun on top, brought up the rear.

Although we planned to walk together, it was agreed that it would be best for most of our group to be at the front, and therefore easily recognisable, in the hope that this would reassure the people in the other groups we encountered. As far as we knew, most groups weren't as heavily armed as us, but we were aware that they all possessed weapons of some kind and we were keen to avoid a "friendly fire" incident.

The morning proved to be a huge success once the four groups we met had recovered from the sight of us being escorted by heavily armed soldiers and vehicles. One of the groups had refused to open their barricades, thinking we had been kidnapped by a rogue government force, until Prince Harry had removed his kit and helmet and walked to the barricade in his uniform to prove who he was and that our intentions were peaceful. This had been a brave move, given that he'd had four shotguns pointing at him.

Everyone we met had been overjoyed (and overcome) at the thought of some help arriving. Once the initial celebrations had calmed down, Jon had stood and addressed them all, explaining why he had come and what he had to offer. You could tell that most of them agreed with everything he said, and once they'd been given satisfactory answers to their questions, the applause he received was an indication that everything he'd said had made sense to them. After all, people were being offered the chance, not only to live, but to thrive and benefit from bringing the country back to life.

They were all warned that the work would be hard, and back breaking. The only reward would be the food and the hope of living in peace under the mutual protection that everybody could offer to each other.

A few people, often those without any family to consider, said that they had no interest in moving, and would take their chances and try to find another group, or even go it alone.

Jon made it clear that nobody would be forced to join, but, given the extremely limited resources available, no help of any kind would be offered to those who didn't want to contribute. A few grumbled, but most could see his point.

We couldn't spend long with each group, as we wanted to get to everyone we knew in the area. Plans for a return visit were made, when more details would be given and arrangements would be made for those who wanted to leave. Having left a parting gift of enough food to feed each group for a few days, we moved on to the next.

Once we'd visited all the groups that we knew of in the area, we radioed for more vehicles to come and meet us at a location we'd agreed on earlier.

We were accustomed to seeing an empty city, but it came as a shock to the recent arrivals, who couldn't believe how few people there were.

Prince Harry summed it up, saying, "It's all very well being shown models and forecasts of how it will be, but walking around in a city where tens of thousands must have lived and only seeing a handful of human beings, makes you realise how many have died or are trying to survive somewhere else."

Walking from one group to another, we showed them how we had learned from experience how to scavenge effectively from every house. We removed drawers to find lost cans or packets behind cupboards, searched for camping equipment in garages and sheds to find forgotten food from a previous trip and rummaged through lofts. We had learned that secret stashes, where one family member may have hidden snacks, treats or booze, could be found in the most unusual places. Even houses containing the bodies of people who had starved to death or committed suicide often yielded previously undiscovered supplies.

These supplies were always a welcome top-up to what we'd already amassed, but we were only too aware that these resources wouldn't last forever. Unless we could learn to grow or catch all our own food, it was only a matter of time before we too would be starving to death.

We pointed out the houses we had marked to indicate that there were dead people inside. We hadn't distinguished between deaths by suicide or murder, but we could all vividly remember what we'd seen and therefore had many horror stories to tell. After a few stories about shooting, stabbing, torture or mutilation, one of the advisors hastily said, "Could you miss out the gory bits please, it's quite upsetting?"

Jon's reaction was one of irritation, "Absolutely not!" he said. "We all need to hear how these poor people died. We sat in our bunker and did nothing, while Tom and everyone else here was facing this on a daily basis. All the dead need to be remembered, even if it's only by Tom telling us their stories. That way their memory will live on in our subconscious. We can't forget what has, and is, still happening. We can't."

Once the armoured vehicles had arrived we continued on our journey. After thirty minutes of slow progress, weaving around all the abandoned vehicles, Jon called a halt. I was in the lead vehicle with him and he called me forward. "The UAV's picked up a small group ahead," he said, pointing to a spot on the map. "Is that anywhere near one of the other groups?"

I shook my head. "No. I suppose it could be one of their scavenging parties. It's only a few miles from where we met them before."

"Fine," he said, and told the driver to move on. I stayed up front so that I could see out of the front window in case I recognised anyone that we saw. The radio was set to speaker and we listened to the continuous commentary from the UAV operator. "You are approaching the last location where I saw bodies on the ground," the radio broadcast, "No one visible."

"That's not unusual," said Jon. "If they're inside a house, we wouldn't pick them up. The cameras are good with both normal and heat modes, but they're not the latest ones, so they only have limited use. Basically, if they're out in the open, we can spot anyone night or day. But if they're in a house or under a thick bush or tree, they disappear."

He spoke into the handset on his tactical vest, "Caution. People spotted in the area, location currently unknown. They're probably from the group we're meeting next, so stay vigilant but calm. Anyone we see is most likely to be friendly."

I could see through the front window that we were approaching a mass of cars that effectively blocked the road. As the thought went through my mind that I didn't remember the road being blocked like that before, out of the corner of my eye I saw something being thrown from an upstairs window of a house close by.

The front of the vehicle was suddenly engulfed in flames, as the petrol bomb smashed and ignited its fiery contents. Jon immediately grabbed his handset and spoke calmly into it, "Under attack, engage all visible targets." Turning to me, he said, "Don't worry, these vehicles can cope with a lot more than this, the only weak spot is the gunner on top. He's a bit exposed."

As if responding to Jon's remark, the vehicle shuddered as the heavy machine gun fired. I wasn't sure if the gunner could see anyone or was just firing to put the attackers off. Visibility was restricted in the back of the vehicle due to the lack of windows, but three small screens in the front showed the views on both sides and to the rear of the vehicle.

Looking at the screens, I could see that the rest of the convoy had come to a stop, and one of the other armoured vehicles had been hit by a petrol bomb, and appeared to be burning fiercely. There were pools of flames around the trucks, where other petrol bombs had missed their targets and were burning impotently on the ground.

I listened to Jon, steadily giving orders for all the armoured vehicles to surround the vulnerable lorry to give it some protection. The weapons on all the vehicles were firing now, as the vehicles manoeuvred round to shield the truck with their own armoured sides. From inside we heard the sound of bangs as if someone was throwing stones at the truck. The soldier next to me said out loud, "Now they're shooting at us sir. Let us out and we'll take it to them."

"All in good time, Private," replied Jon. I was astounded by his self-possession. The front of the vehicle was still burning, we were being shot at and the vehicle was rocking as the heavy machine gun fired short controlled bursts in the hope of finding a target. In the meantime, Jon sounded for all the world as if he was discussing the latest cricket score, but you could see his eyes moving everywhere, as he listened to the reports coming in on the radio from the other vehicles and the UAV operator, and scanned the screens that showed the views around the vehicle. He was playing with a small joystick, which moved a camera that was mounted on top of the vehicle. "Our priority is to protect the VIPs," he said. "I've positioned their vehicle on the side that hasn't been attacked yet, so for the moment they're as safe as I can make them." A flurry of calls came through on the radio and Jon swivelled the camera to face the rear. The rearmost vehicle had also been hit by a petrol bomb.

"Ah, that changes the situation. They appear to be behind us now as well. And unless I'm truly mistaken, those shots we can hear bouncing off the side of us are high velocity rounds, not pellets from a shotgun. So we're facing an unknown number of attackers, with unknown weapons, who have us at a tactical disadvantage."

"So what do we do now then?" I asked.

"Well, we could just drive away, but that would leave the truck exposed, as we'd have to weave around the cars littering the road. Or we could sit here and wait for reinforcements, but they would probably take at least thirty minutes to reach us, and in that time they might get lucky and do some damage which could put us at risk." As if on cue, the soldier in the roof turret cried out and slumped in his seat. Two soldiers immediately jumped up to help him.

He was groaning and swearing as his comrades helped him out of the turret and I could see that he was bleeding profusely from a wound to his neck.

As the others worked on administering first aid to the wound, (basically compression and bandages), he grew quieter and his face turned grey.

Jon ordered another soldier into the turret to fire the machine gun and I admired the man's courage as, without hesitation, he immediately squeezed in and began firing the gun, his uniform soaked in the blood of its last occupant.

The soldier treating the wounded man turned to Jon and said grimly, "Sir, a bullet's nicked his neck, it's bleeding heavily and I think it might have caught something major. I'm doing all I can, but unless we get him to a medic soon, he's going to be in trouble."

Jon climbed out of his seat, crouched down by the unfortunate soldier and took his hand, "Private Eddy, don't worry we'll soon have you out of here and back to your wife and son. It's Max, isn't it?" The other soldier nodded.

Jon turned away, and speaking into the radio again, requested an update from the UAV operator. He began issuing a stream of orders to the men in the other vehicles, using an array of military terms that I couldn't follow, but which seemed to make perfect sense to those he spoke to, as they all acknowledged every direction he gave.

From the little I could understand there appeared to be fewer petrol bombs being thrown from one side of the street so, under cover of fire from the machine guns, Jon intended to lead an attack from that side, clearing the houses one at a time and eliminating our assailants.

Feeling scared, but also feeling like a bit of a spare part in the unfolding drama, I asked Jon what we could do.

He thought for a second then replied, "Thanks Tom, we'll need help from all of you. When we launch the assault, apart from the soldiers manning the machine guns, and the drivers, we'll be pretty thin on the ground. If you could help guard the vehicles and keep an eye on our VIPs, I could release a few of Captain Berry's men to help with the counterattack. That's what they're good at."

I looked at him and nodded. Despite the constant machine gun fire, incoming fire was still pinging off the side of the vehicles.

"If I'm not mistaken, the people attacking us appear to have some military training. They know what our vehicles are capable of, and are keeping out of the way of the machine guns. They're firing the odd pot shot at us from different positions, to let us know they're still there and to keep the gunner moving so that hopefully they can get another shot at him. If we lose our top cover from the machine guns, we'll be in even more trouble. A lucky shot could easily disable a gun or something else, so it's worth their while to keep shooting at us. We need to take this fight to them now. We can't wait for reinforcements."

The soldiers who were sitting with me in the back of the armoured vehicle were checking their equipment and listening to orders, both from Colonel Moore and their sergeant. When the order was given, the machine guns would lay down a heavy volume of fire. Everyone would exit the vehicles at the same time and form prearranged squads to begin the assault. Those of us staying behind would immediately close the door on the VIPs' armoured vehicle to protect them, taking cover where we could, and provide additional security and firepower to help the soldiers tasked with that duty.

Jon stood in the middle of the vehicle, his rifle in one hand and the radio mike in the other. Nodding at everyone, he gave the order for the machine guns to increase their fire. The noise was deafening. At another order from Jon, the rear door swung open and all the soldiers in the assault squad leapt out and followed Jon across to the nearest house.

As I jumped out I could see the soldiers closing the door on the VIPs' vehicle. It was difficult to pick out individuals among the attacking squad, but it looked as if Colonel Moore and Harry were leading the way as they all made for the cover of the nearest building.

The corporal who'd been left in command quickly directed us into our positions. With the exception of my MP5, the rest of our people were only armed with shotguns, not great at any sort of distance. The corporal wisely spread them evenly around with a soldier armed with a modern rifle close to each of them.

Not having a military radio, I couldn't hear what was being reported as the others began the attack. The sound of single gunshots, mingled with prolonged bursts from multiple guns continued unabated, and in the background we heard explosions, which I guessed were grenades, booming out.

The corporal shouted a warning to those of us positioned at the front of the group of vehicles, facing in the direction we'd been travelling when the attack had begun. The soldiers were advancing and our attackers were being wiped out or were retreating against the power of the assault, but we still needed to be vigilant in case any of them tried to escape to the other side of the street.

The incoming fire had reduced to almost nothing as our assailants now had other things to worry about, but the odd shot ricocheting off something metal encouraged us to keep our heads well down.

"There's one!" shouted someone. A man wearing military uniform and carrying a rifle suddenly darted out of a house on our right. I hesitated, not sure if he was one of our guys. Lifting his gun as he ran, he fired in our direction, as he desperately tried to reach the cover of the house he was heading for.

A bullet hit the vehicle, inches from my head, and made me jump and cry out. As I looked up, the man was caught in a long burst from a heavy machine gun and virtually disintegrated before my eyes, a sight I knew I'd carry with me for a long time to come.

"Are you OK?" shouted the corporal. "That was close!"

"Yes I'm fine," I replied, "Just wondering how I'll explain being in my second firefight in as many days to the wife when I get home. She's going to do her nut."

The corporal grinned at me. "Do you mean this isn't an everyday occurrence? We've been bored senseless for months! This is great, doing what we've been trained to do. I've been in the army for years and haven't seen any action or fired my weapon in anger before. Now I've been in two firefights and yes, I'm scared, but at least I'm doing something worthwhile."

Chuckling, I responded, "Try telling that to the wife!"

A shout from the machine gunner above made us look outwards again. A man hurtled round the corner of a building clutching a bottle with a lit rag hanging from it. "Shoot him!" yelled the gunner, "I can't get him."

As the man drew back his arm to throw the bottle, four guns fired and he was thrown backwards by the multiple impacts to his body. As he fell the bottle smashed and, screaming, he was engulfed in the ensuing fireball. His agony was cut short as the corporal emptied the magazine of his rifle into the writhing mass of flames.

"Now I've fired it," he said quietly, putting a fresh magazine in his weapon, and watching the still burning corpse in front of us.

Snapping himself out of it, he said aloud, "He was wearing body armour and carrying a military weapon. Who are we up against? They certainly don't act like people just trying to survive. They're well organised, and if it wasn't for our armoured vehicles, we'd be in real trouble."

"I haven't got a clue," I replied. "But one thing I can tell you for certain, it's not one of the groups we've met before, and we're quite close to the territory of one of them now. I'm very worried about what might have happened to them."

The firefight continued, as Jon and his men cleared the buildings. As well as the shots and occasional grenade bursts, shouting could be heard. You couldn't tell if it was orders being given or demands for the other side to surrender, but the occasional increase in volume, both in shots and shouts, suggested that the enemy was still resisting.

There was a sudden crescendo of noise and then everything went quiet.

The corporal listened to his radio. I heard him confirm the order he'd been given and then he shouted his instructions so that they were loud enough for us all to hear.

"They've cleared the enemy from that side as far as they can tell. They've taken a few casualties, but nothing too serious. Colonel Moore wants to continue the attack while the momentum's going our way. They're resting for a few minutes to get everything organised and then he wants us to help cover them as they cross the road. We'll need to fire everything we have at the buildings over there to keep the enemy's heads down."

He looked at us all in turn and asked everyone to confirm that we understood his instructions. "Start shooting when I order it, but listen out for my whistle," he said, holding one up in the air. "That'll be the signal to stop firing, as Colonel Moore and his men will be too close."

We all nodded to show that we understood. "That gives me an idea," he said, scrambling to his feet and jumping into the rear of one of the armoured vehicles. He emerged carrying two tubes and, calling another soldier over, handed one to him. He had a brief conversation over the radio and he and the soldier walked over to me.

I eyed the tubes. "Are they bazookas?" I asked.

Grinning, he replied, "Come on old timer, this isn't World War Two. They're AT4 anti-bunker weapons. I remembered we had these in the back, so why shouldn't we use them? They cost a fortune, so I've only ever fired a training one, but they're designed for bunkers so I'm pretty sure those little old houses won't be a problem! I've run it by Colonel Moore and he's in agreement. The signal for them to start the assault will be me and Private Pike here firing these beauties."

The corporal and Private Pike spent a few minutes readying and familiarising themselves with the weapons. "Right everyone. Pike and I are going to have to stand in the open to fire these, so when I give the order, everybody fire to give us some cover," and he couldn't help but add "Remember, Pike, don't tell them your name."

A few minutes later everyone was in position, weapons pointing towards the row of houses about thirty metres away, and awaiting the corporal's command.

"Fire!" he yelled. The front of the houses disappeared in a haze of smoke and brick dust, as three heavy machine guns and various light weapons fired at the target houses. The machine guns seemed to be doing an excellent job of destroying the houses on their own.

Out of the corner of my eye I saw the two soldiers stand up, bravely exposing themselves to any incoming fire in order to discharge their weapons.

Both weapons fired almost simultaneously and emitted a loud crack, which was immediately drowned out by the rockets exploding in the houses. All firing ceased as we took cover from the rain of debris that was falling from the sky. Bricks and other items showered down on us and everything disappeared in a billowing cloud of dust.

"Keep firing!" shouted the corporal. As the debris falling from the sky thinned out, the rate of fire picked up. The cacophony of noise was unbelievable, as the heavy roar of the machine guns interspersed with the lighter crack of assault rifles and the less frequent sound of a shotgun firing. You couldn't see what you were aiming at through the cloud of dust, you just pointed your weapon in what was hopefully the right direction, and pulled the trigger.

The shrill sound of the corporal's whistle cut through the noise and after a few seconds all firing ceased. As the dust cloud settled or blew away on the breeze, the scene of destruction we had created materialised.

The rockets must have destroyed the main supporting walls of a few of the houses, as they had been virtually reduced to piles of rubble, and the rest of what was still standing wasn't in much better condition. The heavy machine guns had destroyed the frontages of most of the houses, smashing and pummelling bricks to smithereens, and reducing walls to hole-filled, unrecognisable structures.

"Stay ready! Colonel Moore is crossing the road now," warned the corporal.

Everyone watched tensely as Jon and his men carefully made their way across the road, using every bit of cover they could. As they approached the houses, they threw grenades through any windows and doorways that were still standing.

A squad of six men entered the first house, while Jon and the rest remained outside with their weapons pointed towards the buildings. A few minutes later the corporal spoke up, "The all clear's been given. At ease, but I don't have to remind you to stay vigilant, do I?"

Jon and the rest of his attacking force jogged over to us. "We need to get back right now!" he said. "The injured need medical attention. Most of them aren't too bad, but I'm concerned about Private Eddy. He's falling in and out of consciousness."

Within five minutes we'd helped to get the wounded onto the vehicles, had turned the convoy around and were making our way back to Moseley.

The drivers took less care on the way back, due to the need for speed and quite a few abandoned vehicles were dealt a glancing blow to move them out of the way. Private Eddy looked in a bad way. As far as I could tell, the other wounded were less serious. One man had a bullet wound in his arm and there were a few sprained ankles and possible broken bones due to falls during the attack.

Nobody spoke in the rear of the vehicle; everyone seemed lost in their own thoughts. I could hear Jon speaking rapidly over the radio. He was making sure that they would be ready to receive the casualties, and giving an ETA of our arrival.

Then he was on to the UAV operators, demanding to know why, once again, they had failed to spot the danger before we were attacked.

Looking through the front window, I could see another armoured vehicle heading towards us. Slowing down and stopping briefly, Jon had a quick chat with its passenger before continuing on our journey. He turned and beckoned me over. "That was Captain Berry. He's going to have a look at the ambush site to see if there are any clues to suggest who they were and where they came from."

"I know it definitely wasn't anyone we've come across before," I replied. "I'm not an expert but those guys looked like military to me, and they were carrying military grade weapons.

Why would they attack us without warning and without trying to find out who we are or what we want?

I'm really worried about the other groups we were trying to find today. We were only just getting to know them, but they certainly didn't have the manpower or the weapons to stand up to an attack from that lot. They'd have been annihilated!"

Jon looked thoughtful for a while and replied carefully, "I agree that our attackers were military or ex-military. They fought well today, almost with a suicidal bravery, almost as if they knew they'd get no leniency if they were captured. We only managed to beat them because we had far superior firepower, and could easily flank them due to our numerical advantage. In a normal battle situation, I'd have expected them to surrender and accept capture and imprisonment rather than death. But despite our repeated demands, they all refused."

"Well, whoever they are," I said, frowning, "We've been attacked twice now in as many days and I, for one, am not feeling as safe and secure as I used to. I was beginning to think that the worst was over but now I think it's only just begun."

Jon looked me in the eye. "No," he said grimly, "I don't think the worst has even started yet. The models and forecasts all predicted that the next few months will be the worst. The people who are left now are survivors. They've lived through starvation and attack from others. They'll be tough and resilient, like you and the members of your community. But you're in a very fortunate position; you still have enough food to eat. Your community's only holding together because your basic needs are being met, you've got full stomachs. Imagine if you were running out of food and you suspected your friend and neighbour was hoarding it. What would you do?"

Rather than waiting for an answer, he continued, "Imagine if your whole community had run out of food. You'd tried to beg some from the nearest group, but either they weren't giving you enough or they were point blank refusing to share their supplies. What if you knew you had more manpower and better weapons than them? Would you attack them so that your own children could eat?"

Pausing for effect, he went on "Humanity has a dark side and Mr 'Mild Mannered', who wouldn't say boo to a goose, that 'law abiding citizen', would stab you in the back in a heartbeat if it meant he could steal from you and feed his family."

I nodded, thoughtfully. You couldn't argue with what he was saying. "So what's the answer?" I asked, "What do we do with people if we know they've killed others to steal from them, just so that they can feed their families? Who has the right to judge them, when any of us might have been forced to do the same thing?"

Jon looked at me with a rueful shrug, "That's the moral dilemma we'll have to face." Glancing ahead, he said, "We're almost back now, let's concentrate on getting Private Eddy to Jerry."

CHAPTER THIRTEEN

Private Eddy was now in a serious condition, so Jerry supervised getting him out of the vehicle and into the kitchen area, and immediately began to work on him.

The atmosphere remained tense as I sought out a tearful Becky and the kids. After quick hugs all round I gave them a quick résumé of the day's events. She already knew about the successful meetings with the other local groups, due to the radio conversations that had taken place between us, but she'd heard very little about the attack.

She'd been aware that something had gone wrong, because most of the soldiers had started running around, donning kit and issuing or listening to orders. The sound of distant gunfire and explosions had terrified her. She'd tried to make enquiries, but hadn't been able to find out much information until the reports came in that we were returning with wounded, and for Jerry to get prepared.

Nobody had known who or how many had been hurt, and the subsequent wait for our return had been agonising. Her sense of relief at seeing me step, unharmed, out of the vehicle had released all the pent up emotion.

Looking around, you could see similar scenes involving everyone else who had been on the expedition.

Although we hadn't known Private Eddy until he'd arrived two days ago, he was now part of our group and everybody kept glancing in the direction of the kitchen. We could see Jerry and his assistants, both from our group and the army medics, working furiously on him. We saw Fiona run over to our house and emerge a few minutes later carrying a sheet of paper. Seeing Pete, she hurried over to him. Excusing myself, I went to see if I could help.

"Tom, glad you're OK," said Pete, quickly shaking my hand. "According to Fiona, Private Eddy's in real trouble. He's lost a lot of blood and needs an urgent blood transfusion, otherwise they're afraid he won't make it. I have a list here of everyone who has the right blood group. Can you help me round them up to see if they'll donate a pint or two?"

"Absolutely," I said, glancing at the list. I noticed that I wasn't the right match, but Becky and quite a few others were. Pete and I quickly gathered up everyone with the right blood group, all of whom, without hesitation, volunteered to donate their blood.

With the help of one of the soldiers, Fiona quickly organised the donors and began to insert needles and tubes into the arms of the first few volunteers.

As soon as the first bag was filled it was rushed over to Jerry. We could see him attaching it to a tube that was sticking out of Private Eddy's arm. Fiona filled two more bags and took them over.

On her return she explained to the others that their blood would be taken if it was needed. There was no point in collecting it until then, because it would be impossible to store it.

Harry had rounded up a few of the soldiers who had the same blood group, and told them to report to Pete for instructions. They were asked to wait with the others.

Apart from guard duty, all other duties had ceased, as people gathered in worried groups and discussed the day's events. I could see that Jon was having a heated discussion with some of the government advisors. I couldn't make out what they were saying, but there were clearly two different points of view and neither party was coming to an agreement.

I decided not to worry about it. If it was important I was sure I would find out about it in due course. I returned home to spend some time with my family.

About an hour later, as darkness was settling over the neighbourhood, Jon knocked on our door and walked into the house. The adults were all sitting at the dining room table, a single lantern in the middle of the table providing the only lighting. The main topic of conversation was, of course, what had happened during the day. The children were in the kitchen playing a board game and the only people absent were Jerry and Fiona, who were still tending to Private Eddy.

"How is he?" Becky asked, holding Baby Jack on her knee. She had been happy to look after him while Jerry and Fiona were both busy.

Jon looked troubled. "Not good, that's why I'm here. Jerry can't stop the bleeding and the only reason he's still alive is the fact that he's being given continual blood transfusions. We need to get him back to the base hospital where he can get the surgery he needs.

It's my fault. I overruled bringing a full medical team with us, because I deemed them too valuable to leave the base. We only have only one surgeon at the moment and I didn't want to risk exposing her to any danger."

"Look, Jon," I said, "it's not your fault, it's down to those idiots that attacked us today. You made the right choice at the time and Jerry can keep him alive until he gets back, can't he?"

"He says he can. That's why I need to talk to you. I've asked Pete and Allan to join us to save me repeating myself."

"Do you want a word in private?" I asked, indicating that we could go into the other room.

"No. It concerns everyone so we may as well discuss it openly." We waited for Pete and Allan to turn up, then sat down at the table and waited expectantly for Jon to start. He stood up and began to speak.

"As I've already said, Private Eddy needs to get back to the base for emergency lifesaving surgery. I'm not prepared to lose another young man under my command to a treatable injury, so I'm arranging for him to be transferred as soon as possible."

He paused for a moment and sighed. "That's my dilemma. I could authorise a helicopter to come and evacuate him but I've decided not to because, as has been proved recently, our overhead coverage via UAVs can't be relied upon. A helicopter launching from the base would give its location away and the same would happen here. Even if it landed some distance away, it could still expose you to unwanted attention and put you in danger. Some of the advisers have suggested that, because of the risks, we should all pack up and return to base."

At the shocked looks on our faces, Jon quickly held up his hands and continued.

"Don't worry, that's not going to happen. I'd never allow it. We've made a commitment to protect anyone who wants to help rebuild the country. If we abandoned you, the first people we've tried to work with, that would send a very poor message out to any new groups and to the people back at our base. I've made that very clear.

What I'm proposing to do, therefore, is send a small, heavily armed convoy back to the base as fast as possible. Unfortunately, I'll have to go with them, as I'll need to report face to face to my government superiors, so that we can start making plans for the future. Jerry will need to come too, in case Private Eddy needs medical attention during the journey. Don't worry, he'll be returned to you. He's already agreed to come with us and Fiona is OK with that. The rest of the expedition will remain here to protect your community and to offer whatever help they can."

We all nodded. As difficult as it all was, we knew that what he was saying made sense.

Unexpectedly, Jon turned to me and said, "Tom. I want you to come back with me as well. There are many more people who want to pick your brains about the plans we have, and as we consider you to be an expert, your help would be invaluable. I took the liberty of having a quick chat with Pete before we arrived and he's in complete agreement that you're the best person to accompany me."

For a moment I was lost for words. Thinking rapidly I asked, "For how long? What about Becky and the kids?"

"Unfortunately, we won't have room for all of you and I can't tell you how long you'll be away, because I just don't know. No more than a week would be a good guess. You're under no obligation to come along, but I do think you would be a big help to us." Looking at Becky he continued, "I don't want to pressurise you, but I could do with an answer. If you and Becky would like a moment to discuss this, please feel free to step outside for a moment."

Becky took the initiative by standing up, taking my hand and leading me out of the dining room into the hallway. She turned, took both my hands in hers and said quietly, "You have to go. I know you'd say no if I told you I didn't want you to go, but how could I do that? It would be wrong and selfish of me to do so. The Government needs you. You never know, it might be the Prime Minister who's asking for you!" Smiling cheekily she added, "And anyway, we've got all these hunky young soldiers to protect us now. What could possibly happen to us?"

Hugging her, I replied, "Thanks my love. Who would have thought all this would be happening a few months ago? Me, the expert, advising the Government on how to run the country! It's mind-blowing isn't it? We're going to have some great stories to tell the grandkids someday." Still hugging her, I whispered, "Anyway, from what I've overheard, all the soldiers are terrified of you after the Captain Berry incident. The way it's being exaggerated at every telling, no one'll come within ten yards of your right hook!"

After a quick kiss we returned, smiling, to re-join the others. "Jon, I'm in. Just make sure you keep everyone here safe. That's all I ask."

Jon looked relieved. "Don't worry, I know for a fact that our engineers want to have a meeting with Allan tomorrow to discuss some ideas they have. You probably won't recognise the place when you get back. In the meantime I've approved Captain Berry's plan for dealing with this Gumin character, and he's going to present it to Pete and his panel tomorrow morning for checking. I realise it's a day late but I think they'll approve of it. He's not back from investigating the site of the attack yet, but I've read his report. I think we'll miss him before we need to depart, but I'll keep in constant contact with him over the radio."

More briskly now, he continued,

"I'm sorry, I don't want to rush you, but we need to get a move on as soon as we can. Time is of the essence with Private Eddy. You don't need to bring anything with you, we can provide you with everything you'll need at the base. If you want to take leave of your family, the route's been checked and cleared by our UAVs and I want to get moving."

"You still trust them then?" I asked, a hint of sarcasm in my voice. Having seen a petrol bomb explode on a windscreen about two feet in front of me no more than a few hours ago, UAVs and their usefulness had gone right down in my estimation.

"Only a fool would completely trust technology, but believe it or not, for our purposes, they're more effective at night because they can detect infra-red. We'll be able to see more."

Not quite sharing his confidence, I nodded and went with Becky to say goodbye to Stanley and Daisy. They were very tearful, which was understandable.

Since the event and everything we'd subsequently been through, we'd spent far more time together as a family than at any other time in the past. It had strengthened the bonds between us and the idea of being separated upset them, and me, greatly.

As we walked up to the three-vehicle convoy, the rest of our community, who were now aware of what was going on, had started to gather. I shook various hands and received many good wishes. Pete and Allan were closest to the vehicles, chatting to Prince Harry.

Allan and Pete shook my hands and assured me that they would take good care of my family, and Harry cheerfully confirmed this, saying that Colonel Moore had left him in charge and that everyone would be as safe as houses in my absence.

With a last hug from Becky and the kids, I climbed into the lead vehicle. The doors closed and the convoy departed.

CHAPTER FOURTEEN

Inside the vehicle, Jon motioned for me to come up to the front and sit beside him. Squeezing my shoulder, he said, "Thanks for trusting me and agreeing to do this. Because of Private Eddy's injury I've had to change some of my plans and bring the rest forward. But to be fair, I think I've seen enough of your group and what you've achieved to realise that your model is about as good as it can get. If the decision makers back at the base can get their answers straight from you, it'll speed up the whole process and we'll be able to start saving lives sooner rather than later."

"Apart from Jerry and Private Eddy, who else is coming back with us?"

"I've tried to keep our numbers as low as possible. I wanted to leave as many men behind as possible to help keep your people safe. Apart from the drivers, including the gunners up top, there are ten soldiers in all, twelve if you count us old guys," he said, pointing to us both. "Those with less serious injuries are coming as well. They'll still need medical attention, and as I'm bringing your only doctor with us, they had to be included really. Oh, and I've invited all the advisors along and surprisingly, they've all agreed with alacrity. They all insisted on staying to start with, but then it suddenly occurred to them that they urgently needed to get back to start 'advising' their bosses." Chuckling, he added, "And I didn't want to leave them behind to start annoying young Captain Wales about what he should or shouldn't be doing. None of them enjoyed what they experienced today, and between you and me, one or two of them had a few little accidents when they were sheltering in their bullet, bomb and fire-proof armoured car and we were all out there dealing with the situation. But I suppose that's why we chose to be soldiers and they chose to sit behind desks in Whitehall.

As long as everything goes to plan and we can maintain our current speed, it should only take about four hours to get to the base."

"Four hours! Are we that close?" I exclaimed.

He laughed and said, "Before the event, you could have driven from here to Scotland in four hours and it would probably have taken just over an hour to get to the base. You're already thinking like someone who relies on walking to get everywhere."

Smiling, I agreed, and we talked about how our outlooks and perceptions had changed. I told Jon about my old Land Rover, and how I hadn't felt the need to use it yet, particularly because of the risks. I explained how in the early days I'd found another Land Rover, managed to get it running, and used it to move Jerry, his family and his supplies into our road so that they could live with us.

Things had ended in tragedy when some of the residents of our road had stolen the Land Rover, and ruthlessly run over and killed Ian, another member of our community, in order to get away. Since that time, in my mind, the need for my old Land Rover had been outweighed by the danger of people finding out about it. To be fair, most of the time I'd forgotten I still had it anyway.

The day was becoming more overcast and the sky was heavy with thick, brooding clouds, an indication that the weather was about to change. The light from the stars and the moon, which on clear nights was bright enough to read a book by, was obscured now, and the drivers compensated by using night vision to see. All the headlights were turned off.

It was strange and disconcerting to be sitting at the front of a vehicle while being unable to see out. And yet the dashboard monitors gave Jon a clear view of every side of the vehicle.

The technology was impressive, and you could see how the drivers were able to drive at what felt like breakneck speed through the pitch black night.

Jon kept checking on Private Eddy's condition. Jerry was with him in the middle armoured car which, in theory, was the safest position in a convoy. He was still in a stable condition, but Jerry kept saying that the quicker we got there the better.

I asked about Paul's plan to eliminate Gumin.

"Oh, it's quite simple really, and hopefully it will involve the least risk to us. He's going to send his SAS boys in under cover of darkness to set up a perimeter of observation and sniper points around the factory unit they're using as a base. It's what they're best at doing, and according to the intelligence we got from the prisoner, they're pretty lax when it comes to keeping watch. They don't seem to think they need it," said Jon evenly.

"They're not worried about people escaping. They lock at least one child from every family up in a big room every night and if any family member tries to escape, or even puts a foot wrong, the child is killed in the vilest way imaginable." I shuddered, and thought about my own family.

"Early in the morning," he continued, 'while they're all still asleep, drunk or high, a few of Paul's men will secure the area where the children are being kept. As soon as this is done, he'll approach the main gate in the biggest armoured vehicle we have. Using its loud speaker, he'll broadcast the fact that he knows most of the people inside are innocent and are only co-operating with Gumin to protect their families. He'll inform them that if Gumin and his lieutenants are handed over, dead or alive, in the next ten minutes, the people inside will be treated fairly and offered the chance to live without fear. If that doesn't happen the attack will begin and no mercy will be shown.

He'll give them a list of the weapons they have at their disposal. He's also trying to organise a low flyby of a UAV armed with missiles."

Jon seemed very happy with the plan and asked me what I thought of it. I was worried. "It sounds too simple. These people have been brutalised and dominated by this man and his cronies over a long period of time. Will they have the nerve to rise up and attack him? Will they believe there are still good people out there? They may just think they'll be exchanging one evil warlord for another. I'm not sure, but I suppose it's better than going in 'all guns blazing' which would lead to a blood bath."

"I take your points, Tom. That's why we wanted an outside opinion on this. We're used to planning hostage rescue missions when there's an obvious difference between the good and the bad sides, but there won't always be a clear distinction here. Someone may be pointing a gun because he's trying to protect his family. Captain Berry assures me that his men should be able to get close enough to spot the difference, just by watching how people behave. When the time comes, hopefully they'll be able to protect the people who need it by using sniper fire to take out the enemy, if they can identify them."

Pausing, he added, "Anyway, he's presenting his plan tomorrow and I'll be interested to find out what, if anything, Pete and his panel come up with."

I nodded and sat in silence for a while, contemplating what he'd said. In the end I decided that the plan was a good one and I was sure that Pete and the others could be trusted to help Paul improve it, where necessary. I asked what was going to happen to the prisoner we'd taken following the unsuccessful attack on Christmas Day.

"I've issued the order for him to be executed by firing squad at the earliest opportunity," said Jon, calmly. Seeing the stunned look on my face, he added, "I have no choice; he attacked us without warning and he's one of Gumin's inner circle. I have to be seen to back up what I said yesterday about the new rules for rebuilding the country."

I shook my head. He'd misunderstood me. "No Jon, I don't disagree with you at all. In fact I admire the fact that you're not delaying the tough decisions."

The rest of the journey proved uneventful. Jon issued occasional requests or orders over the radio and listened to the odd incoming call.

In between we chatted about various subjects and got to know each other better. I could see why Fiona and Jerry spoke so highly of him. He was easy to get along with and had a keen mind and a wry sense of humour. Judging by the conversations I could hear, he was also very popular with the men under his command.

As I was still unable to see anything out of the windows and had no idea where we were, I was surprised when Jon ordered the drivers in the convoy to slow down. I turned to him and asked, "Have we arrived? That was quicker than I thought."

Jon shook his head.

"Not quite. We've made good time, but there's no point in drawing attention to ourselves. At low speed these vehicles are designed to run virtually silently, which is a great help in an urban situation. It's the middle of the night, we're emitting no lights and at this speed, apart from noise from the tyres, we're making very little noise. Hopefully we'll be able to pass unnoticed over the last ten miles or so. It's still vitally important that the location of the base is kept secret until we can start the recovery plan properly."

"But surely there are some people you could start helping now?"

"Yes, of course. Sorry, I'm not explaining things very well. My first priority is to get Private Eddy to hospital and I don't want to jeopardise that with any unwanted stops. Before, when we were travelling at speed, even if we were noticed, we were probably long gone before anyone could intervene."

He paused, "But in the countryside around here the lanes are narrow and twist back on themselves, so anyone with some local knowledge would be able to intercept us by cutting across a few fields."

"Of course, I'm sorry. Private Eddy is why we came here in the first place," I replied, feeling slightly ashamed. "But what happened on the way to us? Your convoy was so large that it must have been seen or at least heard by people in the area?"

"Oh it was, and we did plan for the possibility of coming across people. We had a few extra vehicles; lorries loaded with supplies and a couple of buses for passengers. The plan was that if we met people, we wouldn't stop, we'd instruct them to wait, and the last vehicles in the line would stop for them."

"How many approached you?" I asked, curiously.

"None! We saw no one! When we got as far as the motorway, I ordered the vehicles to return to base. The UAVs have picked up people in the area, so we were convinced that some of them would hear us and come to investigate. We'd planned to offer them supplies or, if they seemed suitable or in desperate need of help, the chance to join us at the base. So either by some twist of fate no one heard or noticed us, or they were too scared or cautious to approach us."

Thinking for a moment or two, I replied, "Probably the latter. Most of the people who have survived have probably been subjected to attacks from other groups or individuals wanting what they think they have. Look at the groups we met earlier today. Caution is the name of the game, and talking about today, I hope Captain Berry has some news on who he thinks attacked us."

Jon thought for a second, then spoke in lowered tones so that no one else could overhear us. "Yes he has, and he's requested a more discreet discussion with me when I get to the base. Even if the information he has is sensitive, I'll tell you anyway if I think it's important enough to affect your group."

We continued in silence for the next thirty minutes or so until, after a few more turns, we were travelling down a long narrow lane. On the monitors I could see some people with weapons standing both in front of and behind a sturdy looking gate.

Jon spoke up. "This will only take a minute, they'll have to verify that we are who we say we are and check the vehicles for stowaways."

"That's a bit much! You are their boss after all." I replied indignantly.

Jon grinned. "I'm the one who made the rules and the point the army always likes to prove, is that no one is above those rules. Don't worry, they know that one of their own is critically wounded inside one of the vehicles. They won't waste time and jeopardise his chances."

Jon was right. It took about twenty seconds for all the vehicles to be inspected, enough to carry out a quick search and to satisfy the standing orders, but certainly not enough time to put Private Eddy at any more risk. The gates opened and we drove through.

"Told you," whispered Jon.

After driving for another half a mile or so up the track, we arrived at what looked like a large farmhouse surrounded by the usual outbuildings you saw in the countryside. The first thing that struck me as unusual, apart from the large crowd that had gathered, (most in uniform, but interspersed with some civilians), was the fact that the whole area was illuminated by low level lighting.

It wasn't bright enough to be noticeable in the surrounding area, but was enough to light the area clearly.

Jon turned to me. "Tom, if you'll excuse me, I have a lot of people who all want a little piece of me, so I'll be unavailable for some time. Could I get one of my men to show you to your quarters? I'm sure you must be beat after the day we've had, so shall I come and find you in the morning?"

I nodded and he turned and walked away, quickly surrounded by a group of subordinates. Jerry had supervised moving Private Eddy from the rear of the vehicle and I saw him rush off with the medical team that had appeared. I was standing to one side, watching the unloading of the vehicles and wondering where I needed to go, when a soldier approached me.

CHAPTER FIFTEEN

"Hello sir, are you Tom?" he asked.

"Yes, that's me." I replied.

Saluting, he said, "Colonel Moore has ordered me to show you to your quarters. If you'll follow me please?"

The soldier introduced himself as Lieutenant Turner, one of Colonel Moore's aides. Shaking hands, we turned and I followed him into one of the large outbuildings.

As we walked along he asked me all sorts of questions about our community and conditions outside the base. The outbuilding turned out to be a huge, cavernous barn, containing all the farmyard equipment you'd expect to see. Combine harvesters and a variety of tractors were lined up against one wall and huge mounds of what I presumed were animal feed sacks were piled against another. Everything looked normal.

I noticed that we seemed to be heading towards a small door at the end of the building.

It was a normal sized, wooden door, slightly battered and chipped, and looked perfectly in keeping with the rest of the building.

As he opened the door for me and showed me into the room beyond, I realised that it was actually an extremely sturdy steel door, cleverly disguised. I'm not sure what I was expecting, but I found myself in a small, bare room lined with concrete blocks, with a soldier manning a security desk, and a second very substantial looking door just beyond him. I blinked at the single strip light, which seemed very bright after the subdued lighting outside.

"If we could just sign you in, Sir, I'll issue you with your ID card," said the cheerful soldier behind the desk. Handing me a normal looking coloured ID card on a neck lanyard, he continued,

"This is a temporary one day card; we'll issue you with the proper one tomorrow. Please keep it with you at all times so you can easily be identified. The card runs out at 1200 hours tomorrow. That's midday to you. Please ensure you're issued with the full one before then."

"What happens after midday? I asked.

"Well, Sir," he replied with a mischievous grin, "We change the colour of visitor cards daily. What should actually happen is that if one of our security guards spots you wearing the wrong coloured pass, you should be shot on sight as an intruder in a top secret military base. Seeing as most people know each other here, and to be fair, we haven't had many visitors, we haven't had to test that out yet. I'd hate for you to be the first to try it out, Sir, as you're our honoured guest."

Smiling uneasily and not sure whether to believe him or not, I put the lanyard around my neck and followed Lieutenant Turner through the next doorway. It led to a stairwell.

Looking over the handrail of the stairs, they seemed to go down a long way. "No lift?" I asked.

"Oh yes, there are a few," the lieutenant said vaguely, "but we like to bring first time visitors down this way. It helps you appreciate how far underground this facility goes." As we descended the stairs he filled me in on the history of the base. The section he was taking me to had initially been started in the 1960s and had expanded to its current size over the decades, as each administration had made its own mark on the scheme. The rock it had been excavated from had apparently been ideal for the purpose; stable and relatively easy to dig through if you had the right equipment.

He promised to show me a plan the following day, so that I could get an idea of the size of the whole base.

We'd passed a number of doorways on the way down the stairs and when I'd enquired about what was behind them, he'd explained that there were quite a few different levels containing accommodation, office and storage areas, but for now they were only using the bottom level.

"Why the bottom level?" I asked, wondering how much further I had to go.

"It's the most modern. It was only renovated a few years back, so it was the obvious one to use. It can easily accommodate all of us for the moment, so we haven't needed to open up the other levels yet."

"Aren't the stairs a bit of a pain?"

"Not really. We've been on lockdown, so only a few of us have had the chance to go 'topside'. Tonight was the first chance for a lot of us. That's why so many of us found an excuse to be up there."

I looked up and down the stairwell and asked, "Where are they then?"

With a big smile, Lieutenant Turner replied, "Oh they all took the lift down. As well as showing you the depth we're at, it's a bit of a base tradition for all first timers to walk down the stairwell. Don't get too upset, we even made the Prime Minister do it! We're not sure who started it, probably the few full-time base occupants when they were on caretaking duty, amusing themselves at the visitors' expense. It became a bit of a custom and the one thing the military likes is its customs, so we keep it going. The only person we offered the lift to on their first time was Her Majesty, but when we gave her the option, she insisted on walking down the stairs to honour the tradition!"

I noticed there were only a few flights to go before we reached the bottom. Looking back up the stairwell, stretching above me into the distance, I asked, "How deep are we?"

"Over three hundred feet I believe," he replied.

"I've been told that there were plans to go even deeper as new 'bunker busting' technology was developed in recent years which could have threatened the upper levels, but I imagine that won't be happening now. Anyway, here we are."

He punched a code into the keypad next to another heavy looking steel door and it swung open. I found myself in a corridor that stretched far away into the distance. The décor wasn't utilitarian, but it wasn't exactly opulent either. The walls were boarded and painted a light colour and the floors were carpeted. If I hadn't known that I was three hundred feet underground, I could easily have believed I was in the corridor of a mid-level hotel or office anywhere in the world.

Lieutenant Turner indicated for me to follow. "My instructions are to show you to your quarters and make sure you have everything you need. I notice you haven't brought anything with you, so do you want to go to the stores and get some toiletries and spare clothes first, or do you want to grab something to eat?"

I suddenly realised that in the excitement and the speed of our departure, I'd missed dinner, and was actually very hungry, so I asked him to take me to the canteen first.

The canteen was a huge space with rows of tables, cleverly divided into sections with screens, to give the impression of a much smaller area. Even at this late hour, there were a few people sitting and eating or just chatting.

"Sorry Sir," said the lieutenant. "There isn't much choice at this time of night because the nightshift only operates on minimum staff. There are pastries and pies, but if you want, the cook can easily knock you up a sandwich."

It felt strange not queuing up for food from the covered area we'd created at home, with the smoking beast as the central point. It felt like a self-service restaurant in a motorway service station or airport. The only difference was the solid looking cook standing behind the counter wearing camouflage, and the fact that there was no till at the end of the line.

I helped myself to a Cornish pasty and a pastry, and after pouring myself a cup of coffee, walked over to where Lieutenant Turner was waiting, seated at a table. We chatted about various subjects as I finished my meal and when I'd put the dirty dishes in the correct area, Lieutenant Turner took me to a locked room where he issued me with a washing kit and some clothes I could use as pyjamas.

"Are you tired?" he asked, "Or would you like a quick nightcap?"

"Do you have a bar?" I asked.

"Yes. It was initially designed to be the senior officers' mess, but it's been opened up for everyone to use. We took a vote on what to call it recently and it's now known as 'The Duke of Edinburgh'."

"Why?"

"Well, officially it's because that name got the most votes. But unofficially, the joke is he's their best customer, so it was only right to name it after him!"

"It would be rude to refuse," I agreed. "Thank you, I would really enjoy a nightcap."

Further down the corridor he led me through a set of double doors. There was a hand painted sign above them, a mock-up of a traditional pub sign, with a caricature of the current Duke of Edinburgh holding a pint in his hand and leaning against a bar. Stopping to looking at it, I glanced at Lieutenant Turner and raised my eyebrows.

"Oh, he likes it," he replied, smiling. "He laughs at it every time he walks in."

As we walked up to the bar, he explained that alcoholic drinks were rationed to a few drinks a day. This was standard procedure on active duty bases to ensure that in the event of an emergency, half of the occupants wouldn't be too drunk to help.

We sat down on bar stools and ordered two pints from the bartender. While we were waiting for them to be poured, I studied 'The Duke of Edinburgh'. It was fitted out in a similar fashion to the rest of the facility, but the walls were decorated with military paintings and flags.

As well as the usual tables and chairs, there were a lot of sofas and armchairs scattered in groups around the room, which gave it a homely and welcoming atmosphere.

While I slowly savoured my first cask-poured pint since the event, Lieutenant Turner, (or Barry, as he now insisted I call him), informed me that they had quite a stock of beers and lagers. For some reason they'd received a lot of diverted deliveries from breweries as well as supermarkets in the days leading up to the event! I tried to ask him some questions about the base, but he said it would be best to wait until the morning, as a lot of the questions I had would be answered on the tour I could take if I wanted to.

We were interrupted by a Captain, (I was becoming accustomed to the insignias of rank by now, and was finding it easier to recognise what the officers were). "Hello, are you Tom?" he asked. "I'm Captain Hardy. I spoke to you over the radio when you first made contact."

His name was Ian, and unlike most of the officers I'd met, he spoke with a broad Yorkshire accent. I remarked on this and he joked that he was their token northerner, whose job it was to remind all the posh kids who had joined the army that there was a world outside of the Horse Guards. He proudly showed me a Leeds United Football Club tattoo on his arm. At this point Barry interrupted to remind him about his family's business interests in Leeds which, on the last Forbes rich list, had just squeezed him into the top two hundred richest people in England. So his poor downtrodden northern act might possibly work on me, Barry added, but in the meantime he should shut up and get the next round in!

Ian laughed, shook my hand and asked if he could join us as he'd just come off duty. He and Barry were clearly already friends and Barry dragged a bar stool across for him. I told them about the day's events, from meeting the other groups, to the attack and the journey here so that Private Eddy could get the surgery he needed to save his life.

As word spread that one of the visitors was in the bar, a crowd gathered round us and I was bombarded by welcomes, good wishes and questions about life in the outside world.

I tried to be polite and answer all their questions, but after the day I'd experienced, I was worn out and the two pints I had drunk had relaxed me so much I was almost falling asleep at the bar. Barry noticed how exhausted I was looking and hurriedly extracted me from the growing crowd.

Gratefully, I followed him down a series of corridors until we stopped outside a numbered door. Producing a key from his pocket, he unlocked the door and handed me the key. "This is your room. I'll arrange for someone to collect you at 0900 hours, so if you could be ready for then please?"

Thanking him again, I entered the room and set my bag of belongings down on a table. The room was small but contained a double bed and a writing desk and there was a small shower room. It was very similar to many economy hotels I'd stayed in over the years, clean, functional and perfectly acceptable.

Although I was exhausted, I couldn't resist the opportunity to have a long hot shower and stood for a long time under the steaming jets of water, just enjoying the warmth. The steam and heat seemed to sap any last vestiges of energy I had and I staggered to the bed and fell into a deep sleep.

CHAPTER SIXTEEN

A discreet knock on the door woke me with a start the next morning. Initially disorientated at waking in a strange bed, it took a few moments for me to remember where I was. I blinked and looked at the clock on the wall.

It was nine o'clock. Realising that the knocking on the door must be the person who was supposed to be escorting me to wherever they wanted me to be, I staggered out of bed, wrapped a towel around my waist and answered the door. It was Jon himself, with a few other officers standing behind him.

"Sorry Tom, I thought I'd pick you up on the way past."

"My fault," I admitted. "I haven't worn a watch since the event, and I was too tired last night to set the alarm." I pointed to the alarm clock on the bedside table.

"Don't worry. I'll send the others on and I'll wait while you get ready."

He nodded to the others and they continued on down the corridor, while he walked into the room and sat himself down on a chair.

I grabbed a quick shower and left the bathroom door open so that we could talk. Private Eddy had come through the surgery and was doing well. I remembered with a pang that my family probably had no idea we'd arrived safely. With everything that had happened yesterday it hadn't crossed my mind to contact them. Jon reassured me, saying that our safe arrival had been reported and promising that I would have an opportunity to talk to them over the radio later on that day.

They were due a contact soon, because at eight o'clock that morning Captain Berry had presented his plan of attack on Gumin to the road committee, and Jon was waiting to hear about the outcome of the meeting.

I changed quickly and followed Jon to the canteen, where we had a very quick breakfast, as he said he had a few people he wanted me to meet.

He warned me that I might have to repeat my story several times, but promised to try to make it bearable.

A corporal came and handed him a note while we were eating. He scanned it quickly and handed it back, dismissing the messenger.

"The plan's been approved by your guys with just a few amendments. They've suggested that a few civilians join in as well, not to take part in the attack, but just so that afterwards there are a few faces not wearing a uniform. It might help to calm people down."

He thought for a second and then continued. "I agree, but don't worry, I'm sure whoever goes along will be far away from the action during the attack, and will be closely protected afterwards. Do you think that's reasonable?"

"Yes," I said, slowly, "but I don't want Becky volunteering. She's had enough on her plate with me being away, and I know she'll want to go and help, but there are plenty of other people who could go."

"You can tell her yourself when you talk to her later," said Jon. "Anyway," he grinned, "I'm not doing your dirty work for you. If you don't want her to do something, you can tell her yourself!"

When we'd finished our breakfast and tidied the trays away, Jon led me down a few corridors and through a set of double doors. I found myself in a small reception area. The door on the other side of the room was guarded by an armed soldier.

The soldier sitting at the reception desk stood up, saluted Jon and said, "Colonel Moore, you can go straight through, they're waiting for you." Before I could ask another question, Jon had ushered me through the door, which was being held open for us by the soldier.

I found myself standing at the foot of a long conference table. Seated around the table were the Prime Minister, the Deputy Prime Minister, the Leader of the Opposition and a number of other familiar political faces.

The Prime Minister stood up and came towards me, extending his hand in welcome. Numb with shock, I shook it and tried to take in what he was saying. I suppose I should have expected to meet them at some point, I had known they were in the bunker after all. I shook more hands as I was introduced to more of the people around the table. I knew the names of the leading politicians due to all the television coverage they'd received, but had no idea who some of the others were. Standing on the outskirts of the room were people I assumed were their advisors and secretaries, as I recognised a few of them from the expedition. They looked very different dressed in suits. I nodded to a few of them and sat down.

For the next hour, they questioned me about my experiences and asked for my opinion on various aspects of the recovery plan.

I soon forgot who I was speaking to, and at one point, when I bluntly told the Prime Minister that he didn't know what he was talking about and should check his facts, the surprised look on his face made me stop and collect myself. I began to apologise but he stopped me and said firmly that he didn't need "yes men", he needed people to tell him if he was wrong and he appreciated my candour.

After a long discussion they thanked me for my time and asked me to leave, as I'd given them a great deal to think about.

The Prime Minister summed up by saying, "Tom, Colonel Moore has briefed us all on your incredible story and how you and your friends and neighbours survived this disaster. Now that we've had the chance to meet you and talk about it face to face, we're even more impressed, particularly given that you're still willing to extend the hand of friendship to strangers. In our view, you and your friends and neighbours exemplify what is best about humanity. If we can copy your example, and replicate it across the country, then we stand a good chance of rebuilding something worthwhile again. Thank you."

He began to clap, and soon the others were enthusiastically following his example.

It was all too much and I didn't know where to put myself. Thanking them all, I left the room with Jon and his aides.

Jon noticed my discomfort and said, "Tom, I don't think you realise how important you and your group have been to us here. All we've heard about for the past few months is bad news followed by more bad news. The whole country's been overwhelmed by it. Yes, there may be more groups out there doing exactly what yours is doing, and for the sake of humanity I hope to God there are, but you were the first sign of hope for us. You've restored everyone's faith in our ability to start again. Until you contacted us, it was all just a theory on paper, but now you've proved that it's feasible. Things will never be the same again, but they can improve."

Slapping me on the back he said, "Come on, let's have a break in the canteen. There are a few more people who'll want to meet you in a while."

In the canteen, I spotted Jerry sitting at a table talking with a group of people. We joined them and Jerry introduced me to the surgeon and the medical team who had operated on Private Eddy and saved his life.

Although very weak still, he was doing fine.

His wife and child had already been to see him and all he needed now was rest and time to make a full recovery.

After about twenty minutes, a soldier walked over to Jon and spoke quietly to him. Jon checked his watch and then asked Jerry and me to come with him, as someone had requested an audience with us.

"An audience?" I teased, "You'll be telling me next we're going to see the Queen!"

The look on Jon's face stopped me dead. "We are, aren't we?" I said, slowly.

He nodded, "Her Majesty's requested some of your time. Look, in view of our rather unique living conditions, a lot of the rules of etiquette have been relaxed. She eats her food in here with us, and although she does have the best quarters down here, she spends a lot of her time attending meetings and generally trying to make things work better. She has a position to maintain, but the way she's helped to integrate all the different groups of people living in close proximity to each other has, in my opinion, only strengthened the love and loyalty most of us feel towards her." Winking, he added, "Her team is the undisputed winner of our weekly pub quiz competition!"

Exchanging nervous glances, Jerry and I followed Jon down yet another corridor. He stopped at a door guarded by another armed soldier, knocked on it and entered without waiting for a response. Hesitantly, we followed him into the room.

As if it was the most natural thing in the world, The Queen was sitting calmly behind a normal desk between Prince Philip and Prince William. She was simply but neatly dressed in a tweed suit and the princes were in ordinary military camouflage uniform.

Unsure about what to do next, we waited until Jon had stepped forward and said, "Ma'am. Sirs. May I present Tom and my brother Jerry? You know their story but I believe you have some more questions for them." He stepped to one side and left us standing there, not knowing what to do.

She smiled at us both. "Welcome! Please take a seat," and motioned towards two chairs that were in front of the desk.

Jon cleared his throat. "Ma'am, with your permission, I'd like to return to my duties."

"Please do, and thank you, Colonel Moore."

With that, he turned and left the room.

Jerry and I shuffled nervously over to the proffered chairs and sat down. We were both unsure about the rules of etiquette. Were we expected to start the conversation? Or should we wait to be addressed?

Prince Philip broke the silence by saying, "Gentlemen, welcome. We appreciate that one would normally receive a briefing on what to do and what not to do before being received by a member of royalty. So let me put your mind at ease. The first thing to do is relax. Remember, we're all in this together. Secondly, you're free to speak your mind. Thirdly, please address me and any other member of the family as 'Sir' and the Queen as 'Ma'am'. That way we're still observing tradition, but not getting bogged down in the minutiae. Is that clear?"

"Yes, Sir," we both responded.

I hesitated for a moment, then plunged straight in, "Sir, Ma'am. It's an honour to meet you, but a few days ago Prince Harry told me to call him Captain or Harry."

They all laughed and Prince William said, "I suppose he started with his Royal Highness and bow routine as well?"

I nodded, smiling.

The Queen leaned forward, her eyes twinkling. "How is my grandson?" she asked. "Is he behaving himself? He was chomping at the bit to go on the expedition to find you. He speaks very highly of both of you, you know. He's reported back to me more than once about what you've done. You all have my admiration and thanks for seemingly achieving the impossible."

The three of them proceeded to question us for the next hour, and it became clear in that time that they already possessed a good understanding and appreciation of the problems the country was experiencing.

The Queen explained that Prince Charles and a few other members of the Royal Household were at another location, not by any means as large or as well stocked and staffed as this one.

Charles and the others had been in regular contact, and due to the remoteness and relative inaccessibility of their location, they'd encountered relatively few people, and had therefore been able to move around quite freely outside their bunker, without any fear of attracting unwanted attention.

They didn't mention where the others were located, but I guessed that it was probably at Balmoral Castle, the Queen's summer residence. I didn't know exactly where it was, but I knew it was in a remote location, surrounded by mountains and moorlands, and deep in the Scottish Highlands.

We were questioned thoroughly about the recovery plan, and whether we thought that basing parts of it on the way we had set up our community was a good idea. Naturally we said that it was, and that hopefully, similar communities could be set up around the country, spreading out slowly at first, with each new community reaching out to help build another. The vision set out in the recovery plan should be possible.

I described how we'd been attacked several times in the past and more particularly, in the past few days, and admitted that in the case of the most recent incident, had it not been for the presence of the army, we would have been in serious trouble, and would probably have lost members of our community in the process.

The latest attack had been particularly worrying and I knew that Colonel Moore should have heard from Captain Berry by now, so I asked if they'd heard any news about the investigation. They hadn't, but I'd clearly aroused their curiosity, so Prince William picked up a telephone and requested that Colonel Moore re-join them at his earliest convenience.

Ten minutes later, Colonel Moore knocked and entered the room, carrying a file under his arm.

"Colonel Moore. We've been discussing yesterday's ambush and were wondering if you have any more information about it?" asked Prince William.

Jon nodded, "Actually, Sir, I do. I discussed it with Captain Berry this morning. All we know at the moment is that he recognised one of the attackers that we killed. He was a sergeant from one of his old units. The worrying thing is, the last he heard of him he was serving life in prison after raping and murdering a number of young women. According to Captain Berry, the man was a monster. We're trying to check out the details of the story, but with computer records being non-existent now, it's more a case of asking around to see if anyone can add to or corroborate the story.

"There are currently two theories, the first being that he was released from prison due to the current circumstances, and used his knowledge of military procedures and locations to stock up on weapons with whoever he'd ganged up with. The second theory is along similar lines: he broke out of prison along with a lot of other highly trained, but not very pleasant associates, and has been making full use of their training to wreak havoc. He may not even be the leader.

Captain Berry's not sure if any of them survived the ambush and our counterattack. He found some blood trails, for instance, which might indicate that some of the attackers escaped. As far as he can ascertain, they were only armed with rifles and sidearms. He doesn't think they had any heavier weapons, which is a positive I suppose."

"A positive?" interrupted the Queen. "How can the discovery that they were only armed with automatic weapons and sidearms be a positive, Colonel? Please explain."

"Well Ma'am, we found no evidence of vehicles, which means they probably haven't succeeded in accessing any of our more secure facilities, where working vehicles are likely to be found. These facilities would also contain heavier weaponry, such as machine guns, mortars, and artillery, among other things. If we know what kind of weapons they have, it'll help us defend ourselves against them, and eventually we'll be able to eliminate them."

"If they're on foot," he added, "their speed of travel will be slower and they'll be easier to track when we've located them."

Turning to Jerry and me, he said, "We also think we've found the community we were going to see when we were attacked. The UAV has some good images of the residents. When you've finished here I'd like you to have a look at them, to see if you can recognise anyone. At least we'll know if they've been overrun, or worse."

I nodded to indicate that I was happy to do so.

The Queen thanked us both for our time and told us that we'd better go with Colonel Moore to help him with his investigations. Jon asked us to accompany him, and giving a salute, turned and walked out of the room.

Jerry and I, unsure about what was an acceptable way of leaving the royal presence, made what can only be described as a complete hash of it.

Jerry gave an awkward bow and almost tripped over the chair on his way out, and I gave an embarrassing half wave and left the room cringing, as I knew that it had been the wrong thing to do.

I was sure I heard laughter behind me as we hurried down the corridor.

CHAPTER SEVENTEEN

When we'd caught up with Jon, he said he would take us to the control room and show us the imagery he'd been talking about.

On the way we were stopped by a very out of breath soldier, who explained that he'd been frantically looking for us for a while. The twelve hour passes we'd been issued with the day before were about to run out, and if we didn't get them updated and hand the old ones in, according to procedure, we'd be classified as unauthorised and the base would go on full alert.

He asked us to follow him to the security room as it would avoid a lot of hassle. Jon, apologising, told us to go with the soldier, and instructed him to bring us to the control room as soon as we'd received our new passes.

Twenty minutes later, armed with our new photo ID cards, we were in the control room.

Jon took us through a series of images on a computer screen.

We'd never been to the compound of the group we'd been trying to reach when we were ambushed. We'd met them several times though, and they'd described their location as a farmhouse not far from the edge of the city. It had sounded like a good place to be based, because it gave them access to all the resources the countryside could offer, but was close enough to the city for them to undertake scavenging trips. They'd come across it about a month earlier. It was empty and had been ransacked. The group, numbering about twenty or so, had relocated there as it offered a much better location than their previous base. They were struggling to survive, but had hoped to make it through the winter with what they could hunt or scavenge, until they were in a better position the following year.

They had been the friendliest and most open of all the groups we'd met, which is why we'd chosen to try to find them first and offer what help the Government had to give.

I looked carefully at the images of a farmhouse surrounded by outbuildings, situated about half a mile from the edge of the city. The location looked right. Jon showed us magnified images of the place, using a mouse to track an arrow around the screen and zooming in on the people. Most of them appeared to be wearing military uniform.

"That's not right," I said. "When we met them, one or two them were wearing military surplus coats, but not all of them. Either it's not them at all or they've been attacked and taken over. I don't recognise any of the faces, but then I haven't met all of them."

"I agree," said Jon. "We'll continue our observations and see if we can uncover anything else. We'll mark them as hostile until we find any evidence to prove otherwise."

Jon showed us around the control room and introduced us to the people manning the desks of monitoring and radio equipment. T he CCTV cameras above ground offered extensive coverage and he explained that, as well as the continual visual surveillance, there were motion sensors which gave the operators immediate warning of any movement on the surface.

He showed us on a map the size of the farm in relation to the bunker beneath. As he'd explained early on, the bunker was immense. I pointed to what looked like a quarry on the edge of the farm's boundary and enquired what it was.

"Well spotted, Tom. That quarry is how we've managed to keep this place a secret. It's owned and operated by a government-owned company. It looks like a normal quarry, but it contains a system of tunnels. These tunnels open up into caverns which we use for vehicle storage. The tunnels extend right through to where we are now. All the waste was taken out by lorry and sold as quarried stone."

He paused, as though considering if he was giving away information he shouldn't, but shrugged and carried on.

"For appearances sake, apparently they let off the occasional explosion to give the impression of blasting, but most of the materials removed from the site came from building this base. And as it was a working quarry, people's suspicions weren't aroused by lorries going back and forth all day. It was the perfect cover. Simple and explainable."

Over at the UAV operators' desks he showed us the live feed from the drone that was currently out there. The operator showed us its current altitude by zooming out with the camera. The view was similar to looking out of a plane window at thirty eight thousand feet. The operator pulled up earlier images, when she'd flown it over our compound. It was fascinating and we could have happily sat for hours watching her work.

I asked where the UAVs were launched from. Jon pointed to a large forest on the map, close to the centre of the fields that belonged to the farm. The map showed a wide fire break running down the middle of the forest.

It was, he explained, the perfect launch site. The forest absorbed what little sound the UAVs made on take-off and landing and, unless there was an emergency, this only took place at night. They hadn't experienced any problems so far, as they'd only recently begun the flying missions when we'd made contact with them.

After a pleasant lunch with Jon in the canteen, Lieutenant Turner gave us the full tour, both above and below ground. It was all very impressive and we felt confident that the base could provide much needed help and assistance when it came to rolling out the recovery plan. In the early stages, they would have enough food and equipment for the groups who needed it and in the future they could provide ongoing help and protection. Above ground, although there was no way of showing us the entire site, we were taken to a vantage point on some high ground which gave us a good view of most of the land covered by the farm.

We were particularly fascinated by a large field covered by polytunnels. We'd been using greenhouses already owned by some of the residents and had scavenged others by dismantling and rebuilding them, but they were small scale in comparison, and had only been able to provide a fraction of the fresh produce we needed. Polytunnels could provide us with a continual supply of fresh fruit and vegetables all year round. They were relatively easy to build and maintain, and Lieutenant Turner, or Barry, as we now referred to him, said he would arrange for one of the farmers to come and talk to us later.

We asked him how the base was powered and he told us that, depending on how much power was needed, a few different systems had been designed. There were the usual diesel generators, but even though they had a lot of fuel in storage, they planned only to use these as a last resort. Instead, part of the estate consisted of a windfarm and there was also a small hydroelectric scheme operating from the reservoir.

Once their engineers had replaced any damaged parts, it was hoped that, given the right conditions, the combined use of both would provide most of the power they needed.

"What happens if there isn't enough power?" I asked, "Do the diesel generators kick in?"

"Oh, no. We haven't had to use them yet," he replied.

Curious, I asked "So if you haven't had to use the diesel generators yet and you've just got the hydro and wind power back, what have you been using until now?"

Looking around, to make sure that no one was listening, Barry lowered his voice and said, "There's a nuclear reactor. It'll provide more power than we'll ever need for a very long time. Don't ask to see it. It's in a restricted area and for your own safety, your passes won't allow you access to that area. Even I'm not allowed anywhere near the place.

"We keep it quiet. We're not exactly hiding the fact that there is one, and to be fair, if you thought about it logically, it's the only way a base of this size could possibly be powered internally. It's just that, even though it's perfectly safe and has all the fail safes and safety features built in, people seem to get nervous when you mention nuclear power. The idea of wind and water power makes everyone feel better, I suppose."

At his request we agreed not to talk about the nuclear power plant. Apparently most of the military were aware of its existence, but it wasn't common knowledge among the new civilian arrivals. If anyone asked, they were told the truth. But until then, the policy was not to mention it.

When the tour was over, and we'd walked through what felt like miles of empty corridors and vast storerooms, piled high with a vast range of food and equipment, we asked if we could speak to our families and were told that a five o'clock radio call had been scheduled. Jerry and I both admitted that we were missing them.

We'd spent so much time together in the past months that being apart from them felt unnatural and we were anxious to speak to them.

We made sure that we were at the operation centre well before five.

I let Jerry talk to Fiona first. For the sake of privacy, Jerry used headphones so that only he could listen to the incoming transmission. I tried to wait patiently for him to finish and not to listen in to his one-sided conversation.

Stanley and Daisy were thrilled that I'd met some of the royal family, but far less impressed by my meeting with the politicians, as they weren't familiar with the names of most of them. Becky admitted that she was missing me, but assured me that everything was fine. Everyone was nervous about the plan to attack Gumin's compound, which was scheduled for the following day. The road was a hive of activity as Captain Berry and Prince Harry organised the soldiers, equipment and vehicles they would be taking with them.

The four volunteers from the road who would be accompanying the attacking force had spent the afternoon undergoing some quick military training in the hope that, if anything went wrong, they would have some idea of what to do and wouldn't hamper the soldiers' efforts too much.

They were planning to leave shortly, so that they could be in position by morning. According to Becky, earlier in the day a team of snipers had been dropped off a few miles from Gumin's compound and were keeping the place under surveillance and reporting back. After telling the kids and Becky how much I loved them and giving Stanley and Daisy the usual reminders about being good for Mommy, we said our goodbyes. They were followed by Pete, who had an update for me.

Allan had spent most of the day with the military engineers, discussing plans for improving our defences. With the expertise and the machinery they had, any potential weak points could be much improved.

Apparently Allan was ecstatic, particularly as the officer in charge of the engineers had been most impressed with what he'd achieved so far. And the idea of having properly engineered, constructed and camouflaged defensive positions was making him hop around with excitement.

Once the call was over, Jerry and I waited in the operations centre, feeling somewhat at a loss. Everyone around us seemed to have an important job to do, and although it was interesting watching them for a while, we soon felt as if we were getting in the way.

Jerry decided to check on Private Eddy, and as I had nothing else to do, I joined him. Although he was still weak from his surgery the night before, he was recovering well. Hopefully, in a few days, he would be allowed to start moving around. His wife, Tracy and son, Max were there and I seized the opportunity to tell Max how brave his dad had been and how he'd helped to keep us safe during the attack.

Once the patient was starting to look tired, we made our excuses, and as we were now hungry, we made our way to the canteen to get some dinner. There were many more people there this time and it made you realise how many people called this subterranean world home.

We had the unique experience of the Prime Minister and his wife, both holding trays, asking if they could join us at the table we were sitting at. Inviting them to sit, I introduced Jerry and he immediately thanked him for helping to save Private Eddy's life. He obviously didn't want to talk "shop" so we had a very pleasant conversation about everything but how the world had changed forever and we were now sitting in a bunker, three hundred feet below the Herefordshire countryside.

Finding ourselves at a loose end after dinner and not being able to see anyone we knew, I had a bright idea. "Jerry, I never thought I'd get to say this again. Do you fancy a pint?"

Jerry looked at me sternly. "So let me get this straight. Our wives and children are at home, sitting around the log burner, trying to keep warm as the temperature outside drops to below freezing. They've eaten their meals either in the cold and draughty cooking area or at your kitchen table by the light of a single lantern. In the meantime we've had a hot shower and three hot meals served to us in a centrally heated and well-lit canteen and NOW we're going for a pint in a pub?"

Keeping my expression just as solemn, I replied, "I won't tell if you won't."

Unable to maintain his serious expression, he laughed. "Oh, go on then. But we'd better not tell anyone about it when we get home or they'll all just give up and decide to come here."

As we headed towards the "Duke of Edinburgh", I thought about what he'd said. "But that's the point, Jerry, isn't it? I'm missing home. This doesn't feel real. It feels real back home, with all of us living and working together to survive."

We walked into the pub and made our way to the bar, showing the barman our passes, which authorised him to serve us alcohol.

We ordered two pints and found an empty table to sit at. The conversation continued.

"If, before this happened," I said, thoughtfully, "I'd been given the choice of surviving a global disaster in a safe and secure bunker, deep underground, with everything provided for me, or trying to survive by scavenging for food and having to protect myself and my family from people who would kill me just for what's in my pockets … I'm absolutely sure I'd have picked the bunker option every time.

"But now I'm here and, yes it's very nice and I know my family would be safe … but I'm missing our community. I know everyone keeps telling us how amazing we are and how much we've achieved … but we did it together. I'm immensely proud of what we've all accomplished. It's been incredibly hard and we've had to do some awful things to protect ourselves, but I don't think I'd want to swap what we have there for here. Would it sound strange to say that part of me is actually enjoying it? Even when we know that millions have died and millions more will probably be dead before the winter's over?"

Jerry looked at me for quite some time. "Sorry, Tom," he said, "I didn't mean to stare at you, I was just thinking about what you were saying and you know what, I agree with you. I think it might have been a different story if we hadn't felt as safe and secure where we were, or if we'd run out of supplies. But as things stand right now, I feel the same way. I'd definitely choose our community over this place."

We raised our glasses in a toast and took a long drink of our pints.

"Jerry, I don't know about you, but I want to get back home as soon as possible. We've had our meetings here and we've met the people we needed to see and I'm not sure what else there is for us to do."

"I agree. I've had even less to do than you and you're right, I want to get back home too." Looking up, he spotted his brother entering the bar. He appeared to be looking for someone. As soon as he saw us, he waved and began to make his way over.

"Looks like we're wanted," I said watching him stride purposefully towards us, an aide following in his wake.

"Found you!" he said.

"Didn't know we were lost," I replied, smiling and gesturing towards an empty chair at the table.

"Well this is as good a place as any to talk to you." He sat down, turned to his aide and politely asked him if he could get us another round of drinks.

When he'd returned, carrying three pints on a tray, Jon told him he wouldn't be needed for the rest of the night. The soldier saluted gratefully and went off to join his friends at the bar.

"What's all this about, Jon?" I asked.

He reached into the briefcase he'd been carrying and pulled out a photograph. "I think we may have an answer on that community we looked at today. We flew the UAV over them a few times today, but got nothing conclusive until the last flight of the day."

We both leaned forward and studied the photograph on the table. It showed the same farmhouse, but this time there appeared to be a large bonfire in the field next to the farm.

Before Jerry and I could ask another question, Jon placed another photograph on top of the one on the table. It showed a close up of the bonfire, with a few people standing in a group beside it. Next to this group was a pile of bodies.

We both looked up at Jon. He said, "I think that answers the question, don't you?"

The community appeared to have been taken over by the people who had ambushed us. We had to assume that the men in uniform in the photograph belonged to the same group. It seemed too much of a coincidence otherwise. There were clearly too many bodies to be disposed of by digging a hole to bury them, so just as we had done before, they had chosen to burn them.

"What are we going to do about them?" I asked.

"We?" replied Jon, frowning. "I like your attitude, Tom, but I think this is my fight. They attacked my men as well."

I disagreed, "No Jon. We knew those poor people, you didn't. I think I can speak for our whole community when I say that action needs to be taken against these people, and that we need to be involved somehow. Anyway, we could be next on their list of targets; we're an obvious choice as we're probably the best supplied and equipped group in the area."

Jon leaned back in his chair, took a sip of his beer and thought for a moment. "We need to get this Gumin attack out of the way first. The initial reports are good. All our observers are in position and reporting in, and they've managed to identify most of the ringleaders. The only unknown quantity is whether Captain Berry's men will be able to get into position to protect the young ones in the morning and whether the rest of them will rise up against Gumin. They're fairly confident that the first part of the mission will be a success, because the guard routine looks predictable and very sloppy. The last report stated that most of the guards are already drinking heavily or appear to be high on something. The only problem is that'll make their behaviour hard to predict."

"What time is the attack due to take place?" asked Jerry.

"Sunrise is at 06.48 so they plan to be in position before then. There's no point in it being dark, as they won't be able to see the planned UAV flypast, so unless something changes, that will be when it all starts. After the dust has settled, we'll take a look at this other group."

"Can we be in the control room to observe the attack?" I asked hopefully.

"Of course," said Jon, "I was going to suggest it anyway. It'll give you a better understanding of our capabilities in case you need to call on them in the future."

"Yes, that'll be useful. Thanks, Jon," I said. Then thinking about the conversation I'd just had with Jerry, I continued,

"I was wondering when we'll be able to get back home. It's been fascinating visiting here and I hope I've been of some help, but I'm not sure what else I can do. Besides, I've only been here just over a day and I think I'm already getting soft. All these hot showers, and nice meals and... " looking round me slightly wistfully, "the pub's great! Maybe when your plan's up and running and everyone's above ground, you could keep this place open as a holiday camp, so that people can experience 'the good old days' and get a break from the daily grind!"

Jon grinned at the idea. "Don't worry," he replied, "Let's get this attack over and done with and then we can talk about getting you home. Unless there are any unforeseen problems, I imagine you'll be back in the next couple of days. We've been having a lot of meetings about the recovery plan and the changes we'll need to make to it, and I think some people may still want your opinion on certain aspects before you leave."

He paused to stretch before going on.

"We've also had a requisition demand from the engineers at your place, so we'll try to combine their supply run with returning you home.

"It's strange you should mention your holiday camp idea. I've only just come from a meeting in which one of our psychologists presented a paper and gave a talk about how, in his opinion, people are becoming too used to the conditions down here. He believes this could, potentially, cause problems when we try to move them above ground again. He's recommending a re-education programme of sorts, to remind people that the base was only ever intended to be temporary, and that we all face a lot of hard work in the future."

Jerry spoke up, "I can see what your psychologist is on about. This place has taken people in and offered them safety and security. Some of them may find it very difficult to leave if they've already experienced the terror of trying to survive. I wouldn't mind having a word with this expert of yours to see what he plans to do."

"No problem, Jerry, I'll get the two of you together tomorrow. He wasn't just referring to our new arrivals, though. He was also talking about all the original personnel. Look around us," he said, waving to all the people who were relaxing, chatting and laughing in the bar.

"I suspect I'll have to start issuing orders for most of these men and women to get out there and help with the recovery plan, to work hard, day in day out, living in basic accommodation with an uncertain food supply. I guess it would only be human nature to think about this place and the people left behind with a hint of envy. Yes, if you look at it logically, it's the only course of action to take to survive in the long term. But when has envy and jealousy had anything to do with logic?" Pausing, he added quietly, "I may have to deal with a mutiny as well as trying to get the country back on its feet."

Jon looked away for a moment, then looked at Jerry.

His face, for the first time, full of anguish. "You know what, Jerry, occasionally, when it's all getting to me down here, I do wonder if I would have been better off making my way to your house and just concentrating on helping my own family to survive."

Jerry reached forward and grabbed his arm, "Bruv, you don't mean that. You're the right man for this job. You don't have the kind of ego that wants to take over the world, you've only ever wanted to help people. You always looked after me when we were growing up. If anyone can do this, you can."

Jon took a few moments to compose himself. "Sorry, Jerry," he said tiredly,

"It's been a very long day! And I'm pretty much at the top of the tree here, and I don't really have much chance to offload onto anyone. The loneliness of command and all that …" He smiled at his brother, "and now that you've turned up, you've given me a load more work to do. I mean, we were quite happy hiding in our bunker, watching the end of the world through our monitors and then YOU get on the radio and now we have to save everyone."

Laughing, and recognising that it was a good time to give the brothers some time alone to catch up, I made my excuses, and spotting Captain Hardy and Lieutenant Turner at the bar, I went to join them.

Prior to turning in for the night, (I wanted to be up bright and early in time to observe Captain Berry's attack), I spent a pleasant hour or so in the company of Ian and Barry.

Thinking about what Jon had said about the issues he might potentially face from his own officers and men, at one point I steered the conversation towards what I thought we would need to do to ensure our ongoing survival. I didn't mention the official plan, as I wasn't sure if they knew about it.

Their reaction was reassuringly positive. They knew that they wouldn't be able to stay in the bunker forever, and hoped that at some point they would be able to leave. They were both intelligent young men and understood the need for crops to be planted and harvested, if we were to stand any chance of feeding ourselves in the long term. They also understood that it would probably involve a lot of physical labour. According to them, most of the men were keen to get out there and start doing something. I was heartened by their positivity and made a mental note to have a quiet word with Jon. Hopefully this would put his mind at rest and give him one less thing to worry about.

CHAPTER EIGHTEEN

By the time I arrived at the control centre at 6:30 in the morning, it was already a hive of activity. One of Jon's aides showed me to a chair in front of an unused row of monitors, and asked me to stay there, as it would be the best place to observe what was taking place, without hindering any of the soldiers in their duties. Jerry joined me about five minutes later.

A large screen at the front of the control centre was showing the live feed from the UAV circling Gumin's compound. As it was still dark, the camera on the UAV was set to night vision mode. As the camera zoomed in and out and the operator responded to requests to look at specific points, a clearer picture of the complex began to emerge. Captain Berry's convoy was situated about half a mile from the front gate of Gumin's industrial unit and they were sheltering behind a row of buildings. He had four armoured vehicles and two lorries at his disposal.

The screen also showed the locations of the men he had sent in as observers and snipers. Whenever they came into view on the screen, a blue icon appeared beside them, indicating who they were. The known positions of the guards in the compound were represented by red icons, and as soon they moved, their icon tracked them. It was not unlike some of the video games I'd seen my son play.

"Team A is going in to secure the children," announced one of the officers. The tension in the room mounted, and it all seemed slightly surreal, as we watched two of Captain Berry's men move from their positions, cut a hole in the fence surrounding the site, and then creep through into the compound and crouch down outside a building. The speaker on the radio they were using was broadcasting to the entire room, and I could hear one of the soldiers at another desk keeping the soldiers on the ground updated on the position of the guards.

The camera zoomed in on the two soldiers. The icon next to one of them indicated that he was Private Horine. I remembered him as the man who'd told me to reload after I'd shot the men who'd attacked us on Christmas Day.

As we watched, the speaker broadcast, "Entering now." We all seemed to hold our breath as he entered the building and disappeared from view. The other soldier stayed outside, guarding the door.

One minute later, Private Horine spoke again, "Guard eliminated. Children secure." We all breathed sighs of relief.

The soldier on the ground turned, re-entered the building and disappeared from view.

I heard a soldier speaking a few desks along from us and her voice broadcast over the speaker, "Stay in position. We will advise of anyone approaching."

Captain Berry's voice came through next, "Preparing to move. It will be light enough in five minutes."

Not much happened for the next few minutes, apart from continual updates on the positions of the enemy guards.

After five minutes, Captain Berry carried out a radio check with each of his observers and with the UAV operator. All confirmed that nothing had changed and all was still looking good.

"Moving into position …"

It was light enough now for the cameras to switch to normal daytime mode. The screen changed from a flat monochrome to full colour high definition. We watched as three of the armoured vehicles drove out from the building they had been sheltering behind and slowly approached the security gates.

"In position. Looks like we haven't been spotted yet. Is the UAV ready for flyby?"

"Affirmative, ready to go," confirmed the UAV operator.

The camera angle changed as it descended. There was silence for a moment. It was difficult to believe that the vehicles had reached the gates without being noticed. The guards were clearly very careless.

"Team A, get ready. We're about to wake them up."

The four snipers still surrounding the building, and the two inside guarding the children, all confirmed their readiness.

Captain Berry broke the silence. "This is Captain Berry of her Majesty's Armed Forces. Gumin, we know you're in there. We've been watching you for days."

In the heavy silence that followed, the camera of the UAV zoomed in on the front of the warehouse. For a long minute, nothing happened, and then four men holding what appeared to be guns, ran out of the building and threw themselves down behind a car.

"Sniper One. I have a clear shot."

"Sniper Two. I have a clear shot."

Captain Berry spoke over the open radio channel, "Shoot if they point any weapons towards us."

The men crouching behind the car kept standing up, looking towards the gate and then turning towards the warehouse.

They were either reporting back about what they could see, or they were receiving orders from whoever was inside.

Sitting in the control room and watching what was happening was a very strange experience. We had live video and audio feeds so that we could see what was going on, but we could only hear the radio conversations. You almost felt cheated that you couldn't hear what the other side was saying. We were watching in the third person, observing real life as if it was a video game.

"Sniper One. I can hear shouting, but I can't make it out."

One of the men hiding behind the car suddenly stood and aimed his weapon at the gate, where Captain Berry and his armoured vehicles were currently waiting. The radio remained silent but we watched as the man fell to the ground and lay at a strange angle. The person beside him also collapsed.

The remaining two must have realised that they were being shot at because they turned and began to run back to the safety of the warehouse.

Neither of them managed more than two steps before they too were lying motionless on the ground. The picture was clear enough to show the red stains spreading out from the bodies.

We watched, as one by one, the other sentries were eliminated.

A calm voice announced over the radio, "Sniper One. All clear, no more targets."

This was closely followed by, "Sniper Two. All clear."

A minute later, Captain Berry spoke again.

"Do not fire upon us, I repeat, do not fire upon us. Anybody pointing a weapon at us will be killed. I'm now addressing anyone who's taken shelter here. We know that you've probably been forced into doing some terrible things for the sake of your families. We understand that, and you will not be blamed for your actions. You now have a choice."

"In ten minutes, if Gumin has not been handed over to us, dead or alive, we will open fire. If you hand him over, you will be treated fairly. If you do nothing, we will destroy the building you are sheltering in. You have ten minutes."

Captain Berry now addressed the UAV operator, "Do the flyby now if possible please."

It was difficult to know what height the UAV was at because the camera kept zooming in and out. Our attention shifted to the UAV operator, as she spoke over the radio. She was sitting just a few metres away from us so we could hear what she was saying directly, as well as listening to her through the speaker.

"Descending to three hundred feet. Camera locked to front view."

When I looked at the screen it felt as if I was sitting in the cockpit of an aeroplane. The angle changed as the UAV banked, and we could see that it was now flying quite low, on a straight course.

I was surprised at how slowly it seemed to be flying. Further ahead I could see vehicles in the road, then a few seconds later I could make them out as armoured vehicles.

I heard Jon, who was standing behind the UAV operator's desk, say, "As slow as you can please, Sergeant Anderson."

"Yes, Sir. This is about as slow as it will go. With the missiles on the wings I have to maintain a higher airspeed."

The UAV passed over the armoured vehicles and the camera focused on the front of the warehouse. Faces could be seen looking through the windows.

The UAV operator spoke again into her microphone, "Captain Berry, I'll do one more pass and then gain altitude and return to over-watch position."

We watched the screen as the UAV made a tight banking turn and passed back over Captain Berry. Then the camera turned up towards the sky as it climbed back to its normal altitude. The camera swivelled downwards to continue its surveillance.

Sniper Three reported in, "I can hear a lot of noise coming from inside." He paused for a second. "Gunshots from inside."

The other snipers confirmed that they were all hearing shouts and occasional gunshots from inside the building.

Suddenly, on the screen, a group of people burst from the front of the building. They were bending over and running, while trying to hold their hands up in the air.

"Sniper Two. They're all unarmed and they have children with them."

Captain Berry's voice came back over the speaker. He was on the loudspeaker again and he ordered them all to stop and lie down. Most of them obeyed immediately. One turned and ran towards the perimeter fence. He fell to the ground as one of the snipers shot him.

Everything became very confused, as multiple reports came in simultaneously over the radio. We could see more groups of people spilling out of the building. Most of them immediately threw themselves down, as instructed by the loudspeaker.

One or two foolishly raised a weapon towards the armoured vehicles or tried to run away. The end result was always the same, another body lying on the floor either dead or dying, as the blood ebbed away beneath them in a spreading stain.

Reports were still coming in of shouts and the occasional flurry of shots from inside the building. Paul's plan was obviously working. Gumin's former subjects were clearly rising up against him and were trying to either kill or capture him.

At the rear of the building, Sniper Four reported an attempted break out by a number of armed men. He managed to shoot three of them before they made it back to the shelter of the building. The UAV's camera was concentrating on the front of the building, so when the camera panned to the rear, all we could see were bodies lying on the grass.

Looking up, I saw Jon walking over to us. "Do we know what's going on?" I asked.

"You're seeing and hearing everything we are. I think Berry's plan is working but your guess is as good as mine as to what's going on inside."

As the camera zoomed in on the people who were still lying on the ground outside the building, you could see that the majority were women, and had their arms flung protectively across the smaller figures of the children next to them.

"Jon, as most of the people on the ground look like women or children, you have to assume that the men are inside trying to carry out our instructions. But without any weapons, they're going to get slaughtered in there. Can't we do anything to help them?" I asked.

Jon stared at the screen and thought for a moment. "Yes, we should, but it's not as easy as it sounds. Captain Berry will have to enter a building with no clear idea of the tactical situation. He won't be able to tell friend from foe. It's got disaster written all over it. But then again," he reasoned, "his men are superbly trained and are used to thinking on their feet and adapting to a changing situation. And those inside are only trying to follow our orders ..." He seemed to come to a decision, "I agree that we should try something."

Before Jon could radio in, Captain Berry's voice came over the loud speaker. "Colonel Moore, I think it's reached a stalemate. I'm going to Plan Two."

Jon picked up the handset and replied, "Agreed. Proceed with Plan Two."

Glancing at me and Jerry, he said, "Plan two is the alternative scenario we prepared for. He'll force entry into the compound and, depending on what's happening, he'll proceed with the mission to eliminate Gumin."

Smiling wryly, he added, "Did you think he spent all that time working on it to come up with only one plan?"

Paul issued orders for one of the lorries to approach. It arrived a minute later and followed him as he drove the lead armoured vehicle through the gate, flattening it in the process.

As his men disembarked from the armoured vehicles and the lorry, we heard him instructing the people on the ground, via the loudspeaker, to lie still. They would be handcuffed, but this was for their own protection, and they were not to panic.

I had watched something like this once, in a programme I had seen about the Special Forces. The standard procedure in any hostage situation was to treat everyone as a suspect and secure them. They couldn't afford to assume that they were all innocent, and it avoided any risk of being attacked by someone who was posing as one of the hostages.

We watched, fascinated, as his men spread out slowly and approached the building, methodically putting plasticuffs on the people lying on the ground. Paul must have issued an order not to secure any young children because they were left untouched. Touchingly, many of the smaller figures had now draped themselves across the larger ones, as if attempting to protect them in their turn.

As our men neared the building, the camera picked out a man leaving it, holding his hands high above his head. He was ordered to kneel and keep his hands out in the open. We watched as he was roughly thrown to the ground and his hands secured behind his back. He was dragged away from the front of the building to where a group of soldiers had gathered behind some abandoned cars.

At Jon's request, the camera zoomed in on the group. We could see Captain Berry talking to the man. He then addressed the control room. "Colonel Moore, we have information that Gumin and a few of his men have holed up in the office suite of the warehouse."

"Captain Berry, we can see you, please continue."

"As soon as my broadcast went out, the people inside did try to capture him. They caught a lot of them unprepared and managed to get their weapons away from them, but Gumin and an unknown number of his men managed to retreat to the offices. They've already fortified them, as it's where they keep all the weapons and valuables they've plundered."

"What do you propose, Captain Berry?"

"Let me do a recon and then I'll come up with some options."

A few minutes later we watched him lead a team of four men into the building.

Another tense few minutes passed as we all waited, powerless to do anything but observe the drama being played out before us in full HD and stereo sound.

Captain Berry's voice broke the silence. "Get ready. We're sending some people out to you. They're all disarmed and will need to be secured."

Over the next ten minutes we watched as, singly and in pairs, men and women hurried out of the building, arms raised. The waiting soldiers secured their hands behind their backs and made them lie flat on the ground.

"Colonel Moore, the building is clear apart from the men barricaded in the office. They've secured a good position and may be tough to dislodge. If it wasn't for all the supplies in there, I'd suggest that we withdraw and call in an airstrike."

"Any other options, Captain Berry?" asked Jon. "I agree, I'd prefer to hang on to the supplies but if, in your opinion, it's too risky to remove him by force, I'll authorise an airstrike on the building. The supplies would be useful, but it's not worth risking the lives of your men. You're in command on the ground, it's your decision."

"Thank you, Sir, give me five minutes."

Ten minutes later, he was back on the radio. "Sir, we have a plan. We've got a sniper into position overlooking the office. He's got a good view of the inside. He'll fire through the window and force them to keep their heads down, while we attack them through the front. Let me get the men into position and clear the civilians out of the way and then we'll give it a go."

We saw the soldiers starting to gather up the people who'd been lying prone in the yard. They were moved in groups, and then placed together in one location, close to where the gates had been flattened by the armoured cars.

We received no warning of the commencement of the attack. The camera had shown squads of soldiers moving rapidly into the building and the odd voice command could be heard over the speaker, as he got them into position inside the building.

A flurry of commands burst out over the speaker and gunfire could be heard in the background. It was impossible to work out what was going on and there was nothing to see on the screen, as all the action was taking place inside. Jon was quiet, his face expressionless and his eyes closed, as he tried to interpret the calls coming in over the radio, to get an idea what was going on.

As I listened, I imagined the chaos and terror of a close quarter battle, as Paul and his men fought to drive out Gumin and his henchmen.

"Breach the door!" came through very clearly.

A crescendo of gunfire and explosions made you want to duck under the desk. On the screen, smoke began to pour out of the side of the warehouse. More commands and voices could be heard, then silence.

Nothing was heard for a few minutes until a calm "all clear" came over the speaker. As more "all clears" came through, we all stood and cheered as the tension in the room melted away to be replaced by relief and joy.

"That was a bit tense," said Jon, as he came up and shook both our hands. "I still feel I should have been out there, leading from the front."

Jerry replied, "Come on Jon, you did that the other day."

"You're right!" he acknowledged. "Do you want to get out of here for a while? It'll take Captain Berry quite some time to sort things out and report back, I guess."

CHAPTER NINETEEN

We left the operations centre and made our way to the canteen. It was full of people sitting down to breakfast. When we looked at the clock on the wall, we were amazed to see that it was still only eight o'clock in the morning. The whole operation had taken just over an hour.

Jerry and I sat there for several hours, drinking cups of coffee, and not knowing what to do next.

Our main topic of conversation was, of course, the attack and the fact that it had obviously been a success. We still weren't sure if Gumin had been killed or captured, but came to the conclusion that it probably didn't make much difference either way. If he'd been captured alive we couldn't imagine him being allowed to continue his miserable and cruel existence for long.

What had been brought home to us was that without the extra security the army's presence was currently giving us, then increasingly, our community's ability to protect itself against a large scale attack would be in doubt.

We talked about the fact that we were now in the depths of winter and were entering the coldest months of January and February. Would there be a mass migration of people back into the cities? Whatever food the countryside might have been able to offer would clearly be exhausted by now, so if you had the strength, wouldn't you want to get back to the towns and cities, where at least there was the possibility of a roof over your head and warmth from a fire?

A feeling of unease came over me. "We need to get back home right now Jerry," I said.

"I know, Tom, but Jon did promise he would get us back home once the attack was over. Let's give it time for the dust to settle and then we'll ask again."

A soldier approached and told us that Colonel Moore was ready to hold a debriefing on the results of the attack. We followed him and found ourselves in a room that was set out in conference style, with enough seats for at least three hundred people. Jon and a number of officers were seated at a table at the front of the room. As the room was about half full, Jerry and I managed to find a couple of empty seats close to the front and sat down. Asking for quiet, Jon announced that he would begin soon; he was just waiting for a few more people to arrive. I could see the Prime Minister and most of the people I'd been introduced to the day before, sitting just in front of us.

The noise in the room increased again, as everyone continued their conversations with their neighbours.

"Atten-shun!" a voice boomed, immediately silencing everyone. All the uniformed occupants of the room sprang up and stood as if on parade. Jerry and I, not knowing what we should be doing, followed suit and stood up.

I realised that the Queen and Prince Philip had entered the room and everyone watched as they seated themselves at the front.

"Thank you," said Jon, "Please sit down, everyone. Captain Berry has sent through his initial report and I thought it would be simpler to brief everyone together.

As I'm sure you're aware, the attack was successful, in the fact that we eliminated this Gumin character, who was terrorising and controlling quite a large area. The details may change as Captain Berry discovers more, but this is what we know for now.

After a fierce firefight Gumin was killed in the final moments of the attack. He'd barricaded himself into an office suite once Captain Berry had taken control of the warehouse. Up until this point, the attack had gone according to plan. His victims had risen up against him and overpowered most of his men. We now know that over a hundred and fifty men, women and children were living under terrible conditions of abuse and virtual slavery.

I'm sure as the stories come out, they'll be added to many more shameful tales for years to come about the levels of depravity some humans are prepared to reach.

"Gumin and his men fought viciously, and in the main, without any fear or regard for their own personal safety. They seemed to be impervious to pain too, all of which suggests that they were under the influence of some serious narcotics. Captain Berry was forced to use flashbangs and grenades to make a breach in their defences, and this started a fire. Even though the rooms they were hiding in were burning fiercely, they refused to surrender. Gumin only made a final bid for freedom when his clothes were alight.

Pausing, Jon picked up a sheet of paper and looked around the room. "I'll now read from the report Captain Berry sent through, to prove that I am not dramatizing Gumin's last moments.

"Gumin ran from the room with most of his clothes on fire. Holding a gun in each hand, and shooting wildly, he managed to get virtually to the warehouse door before being brought down by sustained fire from most of us"."

Jon explained that once all of Gumin's men had been eliminated, the fire had consumed most of the inflammable items in the room, and Captain Berry had been able to bring it under control and extinguish it. He was currently organising the survivors, and the volunteers from our own community were helping them to understand that their ordeal was over. It was obviously too early to have itemised all the supplies that remained in the warehouse, but initial reports indicated that these were substantial. Looking around the room again, Jon continued,

"Once we've had time to assess all the facts, I'm sure the survivors will have a big part to play in the recovery programme. They're now effectively the owners of a large, well-stocked food warehouse, and I'm sure that they'll want to help move things forward. And don't worry, we'll make sure it doesn't fall under the control of a madman again. Thank you. That's all for now. We'll keep you all updated on any changes. Now if you could return to your duties, I'm sure we all have a lot to do."

We all stood up as the Queen left and then the buzz of conversation started again. Jon made his way over to us.

"Jerry, I've arranged for you to meet the psychologist we were talking about yesterday. He'll be in the medical centre and is expecting you to drop by shortly."

Jerry nodded. "Thanks, Jon, I'll head over now."

Before he left, Jon spoke to both of us. "While I've got you together, I just wanted to let you know that we're planning to get you home tomorrow. We still think travelling through the night is the best option, so you'll be leaving with the convoy tomorrow night and if all goes to plan, you'll arrive early on the 31st."

"News Year's Eve!" I exclaimed. "That's great! Thanks, Jon. You've got a lot on your plate at the moment and I really appreciate that you haven't forgotten about us."

He grinned, "As I've said before, how could I forget about you? You're the ones who have landed me with all this work! Now Tom, if you could follow my aide, I have a few people who want to meet you. Jerry, once you're finished with Dr King, if you want to join Tom, I'm sure you'll find it interesting as well."

As Jerry set off, Jon led me into a smaller room and asked me to wait. A few minutes later he returned and introduced me to a man called Chris. He was dressed in civilian clothes and looked about the same age as me.

"Tom, Chris has requested a meeting as he has a proposition he wants to put to you. Chris, why don't you start by giving Tom your background and why you happen to be here."

We shook hands and sat down together. "Tom, thanks for meeting me," he said. "My name is Chris Garland and I'm a Bushcraft Instructor. I've been here for about a month now.

When the power went out, I knew straight away what had probably happened. I don't have any ties, so I decided that my best course of action would be to get away from everyone and try to survive in the wild. It worked well at first and I travelled around the countryside, avoiding people whenever I could.

It wasn't always easy though, as before long, the countryside started to fill up with people escaping from the cities. After seeing some terrible things, I decided to cut myself off from all the violence and settle in the remotest and least populated area possible.

Unfortunately, and rather embarrassingly, I was passing close by on my way to an area of Wales I knew would be ideal, when I tripped over a rabbit hole and fell and broke my ankle." He pointed down at his foot, which was in an air cast boot.

"I was now in a bit of trouble, and seeing a farm in the distance I had no choice but to try and make my way there and seek help. Fortunately for me, it turned out to be this place. I was picked up by one of the patrols and I've been here ever since. My ankle's almost better now and, not wanting to be a burden, I was thinking about continuing on my way when all the excitement of making contact with you happened. And now I'm hearing stories and rumours about a recovery plan, so I approached Colonel Moore to see if I could offer my services."

"Sorry about your ankle," I said. "Look, please don't take this the wrong way but, how do you envisage helping us? Bushcraft is all very well, but I'm not sure the ability to whittle a spoon is going to be much help to our survival."

He laughed good-humouredly, "I don't think I explained myself properly; I'm a Bushcraft AND Survival Instructor. Before I broke my ankle I was living entirely off what was around me. I could teach you that you don't have to rely on stored food, and that there's more than enough food to be found just from foraging and trapping."

With another grin, he added, "Bushcraft isn't just about spoon whittling. It's about living in the natural environment, and using your ingenuity and what nature can provide, to find food, shelter and tools. I can teach you to make a great spoon as well if you want, but personally I still prefer my trusty metal spoon for eating."

Apologising for my flippant comment, I immediately saw the benefit of what he was offering. Before the event, Becky and I had created a file containing information on edible wild plants, and how to trap and catch wild game in the countryside. But apart from gathering and harvesting berries, and well known plants such as dandelions and nettles, we'd been far too busy amassing supplies to concentrate on wild food.

"I've mentioned to Colonel Moore that I'd like to offer my services to you," explained Chris. "If we can stretch the food we have stored for as long as possible by supplementing it with foraged food, it'll make a big difference. I could teach the lost art of living on what nature can provide us with. I want to start with your group, then create and adapt a basic survival programme so that we can roll that out as we reach out to more and more people."

It made perfect sense and the benefits of what we could learn from Chris were obvious. This was clearly a skill gap that needed to be filled and the thought filled me with excitement. "Chris, it would be great if you could join us," I said. "Will your ankle be a problem? Do you need it to heal properly before you join us?"

He shook his head. "I'm going stir crazy trapped down here. I can't wait to leave. I might not be up for a marathon just yet, but it's good enough for me to hobble around on. Anyway, the boot's due to be removed next week so I'll be back to normal pretty soon. When are you planning to go home?"

I looked at Jon, who replied for me. "They should be leaving tomorrow, so if you want to go to the stores and pick out whatever clothes, equipment or supplies you'll need, I'll authorise it."

Delighted, I shook Chris's hand again and left him to get organised. My first impression of him was that he was a great bloke who would fit easily into our little community.

"Thanks for finding him, Jon," I said. "He should be a real asset to us."

Jon nodded smiling. "Yes, I've met him a few times now and with the skills he has, he could mean the difference between survival and starvation for a lot of people. I'll need your opinion on what he teaches you, and whether we can realistically use it in the recovery plan. But I don't see why not. I believe he has skills that no one else in this base has, but once again, it's all based on theory and until we try it out we won't know if it's going to work."

Looking sombre, he said, "I don't think I need to remind you that a lot of people will be following these plans of ours. I hope to God they work. Millions of lives will depend on our getting this right, and at the same time we need to be as quick as we can."

"No problem, Jon. I understand."

"Thanks, Tom, the next few months are going to be hectic. We need to get as much as we can in place by the end of the winter."

He glanced at his watch. "Talking about hectic, I've had a request for some more of your time to go over some further plans and ideas we've come up with."

I shrugged and said, "I'm all yours until I go back tomorrow. Could I have some time with you later though, to discuss something that Jerry and I were talking about earlier?"

"Of course, Tom. I'm not sure when I'll be free, but how about we catch up in the pub later?"

He sent me off with a waiting aide to a nearby room, where Jerry and I (who by now had finished talking to the psychologist) spent the rest of the day discussing and helping to improve various plans and ideas that had been put together by a number of aides and ministers. We also met with the farmer and had a useful discussion and a quick education on the use of polytunnels. We concluded that they were definitely something we needed to build when we got back.

We put together a plan for the next few months. The base would remain on lockdown, but we'd managed to get them to agree to contact any groups that were picked up by their reconnaissance in the local area. I argued that they would need to work with these people in the future, if they managed to survive the next few months, and pointed out that they could hardly expect any cooperation from them at a later date, if they subsequently discovered that the Government had known of their whereabouts and offered no help or contact.

Our community would continue to patrol the local area in search of supplies. We decided against actively seeking out new groups or individuals, but if we came across them by chance, we would follow the basic rules we'd all agreed on. We would offer them help initially if they nccdcd it, as a purely humanitarian gesture. But if they wanted to continue receiving help, they would have to agree to the recovery plan and their role in it.

A regular convoy route between the base and our community was being planned. Although most of the soldiers would be returning to the base, we had agreed that a small force would remain within the community as observers and advisors. It would be a great opportunity for the Government's personnel to experience the recovery plan first-hand and the regular convoys would facilitate re-supplies and the rotation of staff as and when necessary. The convoys would also allow us to offer anyone we encountered who was suitable, a place at the facility in Herefordshire, without the need to walk there.

After dinner I got the chance to talk to Becky over the radio. The whole community was celebrating Gumin's defeat. She explained that although they hadn't known any of the people he'd terrorised or killed, the previous week's attacks had left everyone on edge and feeling vulnerable. The knowledge that one of the potential threats to them had been eliminated felt like a weight being lifted off everyone's shoulders.

Becky told me that some of the soldiers had returned to base, but Captain Berry had remained with half of his men to help the survivors begin to rebuild their lives. She also said that every one of the community members who had accompanied the soldiers on the attack had volunteered to stay behind and help.

It was likely that the new group of survivors would need a great deal of support to begin with. At some point the natural leaders among them would begin to emerge, and if they had the will and strength of personality to bind everyone together, then they would begin to function as an effective and cohesive group. Apparently they had enough food, so that wouldn't be a concern, but it was likely that there would be a lot of bad feeling and resentment between the survivors over things that had happened under Gumin's control.

If they could all come to terms with what had taken place, then the group stood a good chance of staying together. As they were potentially only a thirty minute drive or about an hour's bike ride away, contact could be maintained between our two communities, and support could be offered to them in the future.

Stanley and Daisy were overjoyed to hear that I was coming home. They'd missed me very much and Becky complained that they'd both started sleeping in our bed with her and that I needed to come back, before they took up permanent residence and I was banished to one of their rooms!

At the thought of sleeping under a "One Direction" duvet for the foreseeable future, I told them sternly not to get used to the idea of cuddling up to Mom. Then I laughed, told them I loved them and promised I would be there when they woke up the day after tomorrow. After promising Becky that I wouldn't do anything stupid before our return, we said our goodbyes and I made my way to the "Duke of Edinburgh" to find Jerry.

He'd already spoken to his family and was waiting there for me.

I found him deep in conversation with Jon, so I ordered myself a pint and went over to join them. Jon turned to me. "Tom, you said you wanted to talk to me about something you and Jerry discussed earlier. I've tried to get it out of him but he wouldn't spill the beans until you got here."

Jerry grinned. "I would have told you, but I know you hate not knowing, so I've been enjoying watching you squirm. Tom, can you put him out of his misery please?"

"Certainly, Jerry. Actually Jon, it is pretty serious. Jerry and I were talking earlier and the conversation unsettled us both to be honest. It's occurred to us that it's now the middle of winter and the people who fled the cities and moved to the countryside will be dying in droves, or at the very least, trying to survive a miserable existence. If I were them, even if I had no food and barely enough strength to do it, I think I'd make my way back to the towns and cities.

It would be easier to find shelter from the bad weather there.

If that does happen, Jon, then we and all the other communities we know about, and probably countless others around the country, are going to be in serious trouble. I think we'll be swamped by another wave of desperate people, just as the people living in the rural areas were, at the beginning of the crisis.

"Jon, you know we'll do everything we can to help anyone else who needs it, but our community will have to come first. I've said it before, if anyone's desperate enough to take what we have by force, then we'll be forced to defend ourselves. I suppose the point I'm getting to," I explained, "is that if that happens, if the entire country's hopes are resting on us as the model on which the survival plan is based, it'll all be irrelevant if we cease to exist."

Leaning back, Jon looked at me. "Doesn't your imagination ever take a rest? But as always, what you're saying does make sense. The question I think you're asking is: would we, (as in the British Government), allow you to be attacked and wiped out? The answer to that is NO! Don't you remember the basic rules we discussed, just a few days ago? Let me remind you about Rule Three:

'If you fight against the system, be that directly against us, or against any community or individual that is helping and contributing to our cause. You will be wiped out.'

I stand by that rule, Tom. I'll do everything in my power to guarantee the safety of anyone who's agreed to help us."

I looked at the determination on his face and felt better. "Thank you, Jon. That means a lot. I know Allan's put in a request for better weapons, to improve our defence capability. I suppose it's even more important now that we've come across that group that attacked us. I think we're all starting to realise that we would have been in real danger if it hadn't been for you and your men. We can't rely on you being there to defend us every time."

"Tom, if you think I'm going to start the United Kingdom's first armed militia since they were absorbed into the British Army by the 1907 Territorial and Reserve Forces Act then you've got another think coming!"

I opened my mouth to protest, but he held up his hand to keep me quiet.

"But if you're asking me if I've been given the authority by the Head of the United Kingdom's Armed Forces to issue restricted weaponry to a selected few people in order to assist in the recovery plan, then the answer is yes," he added calmly. "You'll also have the added security of the permanent force we've agreed to maintain at your location."

I began to smile and relief washed over me. "Allan will be very happy."

"Yes, I imagine he will be," retorted Jon, grinning. "We'll have to be very careful about issuing weapons to other groups, though. I know I can trust you to use them purely in defence. I'm not sure any other group will gain sufficient trust to be issued with any."

Jerry spoke up. "I agree with Tom. You know our views on firearms differ. It was Tom who insisted I take the weapons out of that crate you sent me and he was the one who showed me how to use them. Since then I've shot at and probably killed a number of people in self-defence. Those times it was the only way to save the community. So for now I agree that guns are a necessary evil. But I hope they'll be a short-lived one."

Jon nodded. "For the time being, it's going to be impossible to police the use of them, but maybe in the future, when, hopefully things are returning to normal, we can start to reintroduce a form of gun control."

Jerry interrupted. He was looking at me. "That's exactly it, Tom. That look of disappointment on your face at the thought of your nice shiny machine gun being taken away from you, is why we're going to need gun control. I'd trust you with my life and the lives of my family, but before the event you would never have considered owning a machine gun, because in our society, with its tightly controlled gun ownership, it wasn't necessary. Now, on the other hand, we need weapons to protect ourselves. Tom, if, hopefully, in the future they're not needed, would you be happy to hand yours back?"

I did think about answering with the phrase, "I'll give you my gun when you pry it from my cold, dead hands," but thought better of it. I thanked Jon for his offer of weapons and hastily changed the subject, knowing that Jerry would probably beat any argument I put forward, because "cos I want it" didn't exactly constitute a good argument.

Jon told us about the equipment the engineers had requested for the convoy, to help reinforce our defences. Most of it consisted of sheets and rolls of fencing and razor wire but there were a few items that mystified us, as we couldn't begin to identify what they were for. It was agreed that in the morning we would help load up the convoy, so that we could see what was being sent and at the same time, add any other items we thought necessary.

We thanked him for his generosity, and he shrugged and said, "We have mountains of equipment here. A lot of it was stored according to the whim of whatever official was in charge at the time. It's not doing anyone any good here. All right, it probably won't last forever and maybe this is selfish, but if it's going to be used by anyone I'd rather it was used to keep my family safe."

I asked if a decision had been reached about how to deal with the group at the farmhouse. "We've had a few ideas. The best one so far has come from Sergeant Anderson, one of the UAV operators, following yesterday's attack. It's quite simple really. We've been monitoring them since we found their location. Since they ambushed us, they've rarely ventured far from their base. They're probably licking their wounds and planning their next move. If they've got enough supplies at their location they won't need to stray too far.

At night, apart from the men on guard duty, they all bunk down in the main farmhouse. Given the risks associated with launching an assault on a well-armed and well trained force in a defensible location, we're considering using a UAV to launch a missile strike against them. It would flatten most of the compound, and if we followed it up with a ground attack to mop up any survivors, that should, in theory, be sufficient to eliminate that threat and reduce the likelihood of heavy casualties on our side."

We agreed that it sounded like a good plan and moved on to a discussion about the use of state of the art air to ground missiles in the British Isles.

We finished the day with another pleasant evening in the surreal world of Britain's (and possibly the world's) only working pub.

CHAPTER TWENTY

The next day passed in a blur, as we were called into last minute meetings and we helped to load up the lorries with all the supplies we would be returning with. The plan was for the convoy to depart via the quarry exit, where the underground caverns, used for storing most of the heavy lorries and vehicles, were situated.

Most of the stuff was obviously construction equipment, which I imagined the engineers would be using to improve our defences, but some of the items intrigued me. As I helped to push a large trailer into position so that it could be hooked up to the towing hitch of a lorry, I asked what was in the trailer. Barry, who much to his delight, was going to be travelling with the convoy and then staying behind with us, explained that it was a mobile shower unit.

"Colonel Moore gave orders for it to be included after you made that comment about the luxury of having hot showers every day. He thought it only fair that the rest of your community should experience it too. We'll have to work out the logistics, and whether or not it's possible for it to be used in the long term."

"Why? What's the problem?" Jerry asked.

"It uses gas or electricity to heat the water. Bottles of gas and the fuel needed to power a generator are limited resources. So the question we have to ask ourselves is: is it a luxury or a necessity? And is it really worth using valuable resources to operate it?"

"I wouldn't worry," grinned Jerry. "You haven't met Russ, our resident boffin, yet. Of course a daily shower's a luxury, but if anyone can work out a sustainable way of making it work, he can."

I joined in, "We could open up a spa retreat. We've got Kim to give us all massage therapy and now we've got hot running showers! If we had any neighbours they'd be really jealous."

Barry, who was concentrating on getting the vehicles loaded up as quickly as possible so as not to delay our departure, gave no response. We concentrated next on loading up the weapons we had been allocated.

As we loaded the crates on to one of the vehicles, he told us what they were. We were being given SA80 assault weapons and Light Machine Guns. He explained that once we'd been trained on how to use them, the SA80s would be excellent weapons for personal defence on our scavenging missions. The variants we were getting were the latest in military technology. The Light Machine Guns would greatly improve our defensive capabilities, and the intention was to keep a few strategically placed around our compound.

Other such goodies included enough tactical vests and helmets to kit out every adult at the compound. These would provide much better protection than the standard police issue kits we'd been wearing up until now, and they would make it easier to carry spare magazines for the weapons we were getting. They were also giving us some night vision goggles for our night time sentries to use.

As he stacked up boxes of ammunition, he explained that both weapons used the standard 5.56mm NATO rounds and that the amount we were getting would be more than enough for our training needs and initial use. I had also asked for, and received, a large quantity of 9mm ammunition for the MP5s Jerry and I owned. We still had a fair amount of ammunition left, but as they were on offer, I thought it sensible to stock up on as much as we could.

We all hoped that we wouldn't have to use the weapons, but just having them made us feel safer.

If someone did decide to attack us, then unless they outnumbered us, or had far superior weaponry, we should hopefully be more than capable of protecting ourselves.

I was introduced to the soldiers and civilian volunteers who would be relieving the personnel at our community (the current personnel would be returning to the base when the convoy came back). Before winter was over, the plan was to give people on the base (both civilian and military), the opportunity to experience life on the outside, to give them an idea of what to expect in the future. The ten civilians, all men, had arrived separately at the base over the past few months.

Barry explained that the volunteers had all been chosen for their ability to survive reasonably well on the outside prior to finding the base, and for passing all the entry requirements.

Although no one was quite as experienced as Chris Garland, they had all used a variety of bushcraft and survival skills to survive.

It was hoped that once they had spent time with us, and learned more from Chris, they could be used to help train and prepare others for life off the base.

I hoped that the people in our road would see past the possible inconveniences that might arise from our being treated like a tourist attraction. Having to greet and give guided tours to a constant influx of visitors would probably interrupt some of us in our daily chores, and there was a concern that the presence of other people might upset the existing dynamics of our community.

Although we had been assured that we would receive help whenever we needed it, I decided we would have a full community meeting when we got back. Within the space of a week, we'd gone from surviving completely on our own, to having all the help and protection that the British Government could offer us.

The needs, wants and expectations of everyone in the group would undoubtedly have changed.

Before Jon's visit, we'd all worked together towards a common goal - survival. Now that it looked as if our survival was assured, (we were, after all, the community on which the "blueprint for survival" would be based), would we still be united?

I had to stop myself. In my mind I was now questioning whether contacting Jon had been the right thing to do. I shook myself impatiently. Of course it was! How could it not be? Even if Gumin's men hadn't managed to get us, I was damn sure that sooner or later the renegade soldiers would have found us, and they would almost certainly have overwhelmed us, with devastating consequences.

Chris, the Bushcraft Instructor, was helping out as well. In spite of his ankle, he'd refused any help and insisted on carrying and loading boxes that were as heavy as everyone else's. It was only when Jerry virtually ordered him to stop, saying that he would be extending his recovery time unless he rested it, that he conceded defeat.

We found him a job checking off items on a list, to ensure that nothing was forgotten.

Once the vehicles were fully loaded and double checked, there wasn't much left to do apart from rest and wait for nightfall so that we could start our journey. We were instructed to assemble at ten o'clock, with the aim of leaving at midnight. We should then arrive at the compound at four or five in the morning. The soldiers went off to say goodbye to their families, or to get some sleep, as they knew they were unlikely to get any later.

Jerry and I knew that there wasn't much chance of us sleeping, and not wanting to interrupt the others while they were working, we packed the belongings we'd acquired since our arrival and went along to the canteen to have some food and to wait until it was time to leave. As the canteen and the pub were the hub of the base and word had spread that we were leaving, we had a continual procession of people wanting to wish us good luck and farewell.

Jon came to find us before it was time to leave, and he and Jerry had a few minutes together saying their goodbyes, before we walked through the maze of passages that eventually led to the garage area of the mine system.

The cavern from which the convoy would be leaving was an impressive sight. The "secret underground base", harshly lit by industrial lighting, its walls lined with tanks and other deadly looking vehicles, and with soldiers hurrying back and forth, reminded me of a scene from a James Bond movie. If Bond himself had suddenly abseiled from the ceiling with the intention of interrupting some evil villain's plans for world domination, he probably wouldn't have looked out of place.

Shaking Jon's hand, I got into the first armoured vehicle and waited for Jerry to climb on board. As we were leaving at night, we would be travelling without lights, using night vision.

To adjust everyone's eyes to the darkness, once all unnecessary personnel had left the cavern, all the lights were switched off. The standard procedure was to wait for thirty minutes, to give the human eye the optimum time to adjust to the conditions. We sat patiently in the vehicle, a small red light providing the only illumination. It was good practice to get everyone's eyes to their optimum night vision. If we encountered a problem, or were attacked and had to leave the vehicle, good night vision could mean the difference between life and death.

Once the thirty minutes were up and the all clear had been given by the UAV operator and the sentries patrolling the perimeter, the vehicles started up their engines. After a last good luck message from Colonel Moore, the convoy exited the caverns and began the journcy homc.

Travelling in the back of the vehicle meant that there were no external reference points, so we were reliant upon the driver or Lieutenant Turner to update us on the journey's progress.

After the initial slow and silent drive through the area just outside the base it was a relief to pick up speed. Although I'd only been away a few days, I could feel the excitement building at the thought of seeing my family again.

It was an uneventful journey and as always, when you are excited about reaching your destination, it seemed to take hours longer than the journey we'd made to the base a few days before.

Barry turned to us. "Ten minutes, guys. I've just spoken to them and they know we're close."

Jerry, who was just as excited as I was, grinned at me. I asked the soldier who was sitting next to me what the time was. It was half past four in the morning. We leaned forward and tried to peer through the darkness ahead of us. As the vehicle slowed to a halt and Barry spoke to someone outside, we stood up. Looking at us he smiled and said, "We're here. Give us thirty seconds to get through the perimeter and parked up, and then you can get out."

When the engines stopped and the rear doors opened, Jerry and I were the first to exit the vehicle. The temporary lights on the road had been turned on and we blinked as our eyes adjusted to the bright light. Looking around, I saw Becky, Stanley and Daisy standing there. They were looking at me, but as I was wearing full military kit and helmet, they hadn't recognised me. It was only when I called their names and waved at them that they realised who I was. Stanley and Daisy immediately launched themselves at me, shouting "Daddy!" and hugged me just as fiercely as I was hugging them. Becky stepped forward a little more sedately and gave me a quick kiss, conscious that all the soldiers and civilians disembarking from the vehicles were staring at us. Ignoring them, and accompanied by a few cheers and an "Uurggh dad!" from my children, I grabbed her, gave her a big kiss and whispered "missed you!" in her ear. Jerry and Fiona, I noticed, were doing the same.

When I finally looked round, a crowd was gathering. The excitement of another arrival on the road had brought most people out early to greet us. Prince Harry and Captain Berry walked over, and after an exchange of salutes with the new arrivals, they turned to us and shook our hands.

There was a cold wind blowing and the temperature was below freezing, so I suggested that we at least go and shelter in the kitchen area. As I walked down the road, holding my children's hands, I suddenly realised how tired I was. I was home, and the adrenaline and excitement that had kept me awake drained from my body. Turning to Harry and Paul, I told them I would grab a few hours' sleep and catch up with them in the morning.

I knew I probably wouldn't sleep, but at least I could spend some time with my family before throwing myself back into the life of the community.

I spent a happy couple of hours cuddling up and chatting to the kids and Becky, until early in the morning, Stanley and Daisy finally drifted off to sleep, exhausted after all the excitement. Becky and I spent a quiet hour together before venturing out to the kitchen area.

CHAPTER TWENTY ONE

Although I'd only been away for a few days, it felt good to be back. As dawn broke and the day grew lighter, I could already see that a few changes had been made. The kitchen and eating area had been expanded and reorganised, most likely to create more space to cater for our greatly expanded population. It all looked a bit more solid and better built than before. Light fittings hung from the ceiling rafters and a log burner had been installed. Even though it was cold and blustery outside, it felt reasonably warm and cosy.

The log burner looked familiar and I realised that it was the one from the "Prince of Wales" pub at the top of the road. It was an impressive looking thing and had been used to heat their large outside area. From memory, it had also kicked out a lot of heat. No wonder it felt warm in there.

I sat at a table eating my breakfast, and it felt good to see all the familiar and friendly faces again. I'd spent some time catching up with everyone. Pete and Allan walked in and came over to join me. Allan still looked like one of the happiest men on Earth, and when I mentioned Michelle his smile got even bigger. They filled me in on what had happened in the last few days. The main event had obviously been the attack on Gumin. Pete had already met with the newly elected leader of the group.

The group still had a lot of issues to deal with. A number of families and individuals had left the community, either unwilling or unable to forgive and forget what had happened. Pete thought that those who remained stood a chance of making a workable community. The warehouse had offered up an impressive amount of supplies and food so that was the least of their worries.

The army had rebuilt their fences and Pete and Captain Berry were helping them out with their security arrangements. It would be hard work for them, particularly given the circumstances that had brought them all together, but Pete had faith that with the right support, they would get there.

Allan was delighted about the plans for improving our defences and had nothing but praise for the army engineers. The improvements to the kitchen area had only taken just over a day, and they had all worked well together. Some of the work had already been done on the defences, but he was eager to see if we'd brought along the supplies that the engineers had asked for, and was looking forward to starting the work as soon as possible. When I mentioned the weapons Jon had allowed us to have, he got so excited I thought he was going to dance a jig on the tables.

I steered the conversation around to something that had occurred to me the day before, when I'd met the new visitors we were going to host. Given all the extra help we were now receiving from the British Government, both in supplies and manpower, would our needs, wants and expectations, as individuals and as a group, change? Would we still be able to hold together as a united group?

Pete looked pensive for a while and then nodded at me and changed the subject. As it was New Year's Eve, in my absence, the community had voted to invite the nearest groups to join us in marking the passing of another year. The majority of the people in these groups were taking up Jon's offer and were planning to return to the base and help to start the recovery. We'd got to know some of them reasonably well over the past few months, so it would be a farewell party as well.

They'd received no confirmation of a leaving date as yet. The ambush we'd experienced and the attack on Gumin had taken up a lot of the planners' valuable time, but they'd received assurances that the offer still stood and would happen as soon as possible.

Pete planned to keep the same rotas as on Christmas Day. We would still maintain the sentries but he would arrange for the shifts to be shorter to give everyone a chance to join in.

All the groups that had accepted the invitation to the New Year party had been told to arrive any time after four pm. They would be welcome to stay as long as they wanted, and if they didn't feel able to return to their location we would find a bed or couch for them to sleep on.

By now most of the community had gathered in the kitchen area, and as had become the tradition, Pete allocated everyone's daily tasks. Scavenging had been suspended since the recent attacks while we concentrated on improving our defences.

Apart from the people allocated to kitchen, sentry or woodcutting duties, everyone else was working with Allan and the soldiers. The morning classes had also been suspended for the day, so Pete organised the eager children into various groups and sent them off on useful tasks which would keep them from getting under our feet.

Spotting Chris Garland, I beckoned him over and introduced him to Pete and Allan. I'd told them all about him in a previous radio conversation, and they'd agreed that having him here was a great idea. I asked him if he wanted to join me on the tour I was arranging for the new arrivals.

"I'd love to," he said, "But my ankle's throbbing after yesterday and Jerry's just caught me hobbling as I was making my way here. He called me an idiot and told me if I didn't rest it today and take some anti-inflammatories, he'd ground me for even longer, so I'm stuck here."

Pete replied, "Don't worry Chris, it just means you're stuck with me. I need to have a chat with you about how you want to run these training courses. If we can start planning them now, I can reorganise the rotas to make sure they're scheduled in."

"Scheduled in? It all sounds very efficient here."

As Allan and I left to start the day's tasks, I waited until I was out of accurate throwing range and turned to them both.

"Don't worry, Chris, you'll soon realise how it works around here. General Pete's only happy when he knows all his subjects are working themselves into an early grave."

As I pretended to run for cover, I heard Pete shouting comments such as "monkey" and "organ grinder" and "dog" and "bark".

Prince Harry accompanied me on the tour. While I showed the ten new arrivals around the entire compound and the area just outside the walls, I ran through the different routines and the jobs that we were expected to do.

Harry did the same with the soldiers, describing how the two groups of civilians and military personnel cooperated and worked together. He gave them instructions about the expected code of conduct and how, for the sake of harmony between the two groups, things ran slightly differently to how they usually did on a military base.

Once the tour was completed, Harry and I and the visitors went to help Allan.

Improvements had been made to the main perimeter fence over the last day or two, by adding extra coils of razor wire. Further refinements were planned, but the first major change would be to the row of cars we'd used as our first line of defence all those months ago. It had proved a success and helped us fight off the first attack by the gang from St Agnes Rd. But it had also made a useful barrier for our hostile visitors on Christmas Day to hide behind.

The proposal was to remove the cars from both ends of the road and replace them with an anti-climb wire fence, topped with razor wire. Aware that there was a large quantity in storage at the base, the engineers had lost no time in requesting that it be included in the convoy. We would have a clear view of the road and it would make it much harder for anyone to approach unseen. Removing the cars would be easy given the extra help we had on hand, but careful thought would have to be given to where the cars should be removed to, as Allan didn't want them carelessly dumped in the wrong place.

The tools the engineers had brought with them made the job of digging post holes easy, and in no time at all, posts were being driven into the ground and fixed with the remaining bags of fast-setting post-fix I'd ordered just before the EMP hit.

The cold wind was really biting and there was an occasional flurry of snow. Without the advantage of weather forecasting, which now consisted of looking out of the window every morning to see what the weather was doing, it felt as if a proper snow fall might be on the way. Even with the heat generated by hard work and the hot drinks we had on our brief rest breaks, we were all shivering, and it made us wonder how people less fortunate than ourselves would be faring now that winter was really taking hold.

Everyone worked furiously to get the fence finished before the end of the day, and finally, just before the first neighbouring group arrived, we all stood back to admire our work.

Without ladders, the fence was a virtually unscalable barrier and looked very impressive. It was forbidding enough to be a deterrent in its own right. It was a shame that there wasn't enough of it available to encircle us completely.

As the first guests began to arrive, the work stopped, and after a quick wash and change, we all congregated in the kitchen area, if not to celebrate, then to mark the passing of the year that had changed the world forever.

The evening was a great success and proved that you cannot repress the human spirit. We'd forged a new way of life after the world had slipped into darkness and we'd lost friends and been forced to kill in order to protect ourselves. We'd made new friends and created communities to help protect each other and stand together against all the known and unknown dangers we would be facing in the future. We lived life on the edge, constantly looking over our shoulders, always expecting a new problem or danger to arise. It was difficult to relax, as you never knew when you'd be called upon to defend your community. When I thought about it, we should all have been nervous wrecks!

But in spite of it all, once you had a group of people together in one room, and you gave them a secure environment, even if some of them were strangers, the natural human need for interaction took over and the fun began (helped by a liberal application of alcohol!)

The kitchen area was alive with conversation and laughter. Although the cold wind occasionally found its way in, it did nothing to dampen anyone's spirits and soon hidden talents were emerging, musical instruments were appearing and an impromptu band startcd up. The singing was as enthusiastic as the playing and a great time was had by all.

The only time the mood became sombre was just before midnight, when Prince Harry stood up and called for silence. He asked for a minute of reflection or prayer before the clock struck twelve. Families gathered together, held hands or hugged, and it wasn't long before tears were streaming down everyone's faces, as lost loved ones were remembered.

For the first time since the BBC had first broadcast it, in 1923, the New Year wasn't marked by the chiming of Big Ben. Instead, Prince Harry, in his ceremonial uniform, fired his pistol into the air. The gunshot snapped us out of our sombre mood, and determined to find joy out of the sorrow we were feeling, we all launched into several choruses of "Auld Lang Syne", which became louder and more raucous every time we sang it.

Nobody seemed to want the party to end, perhaps because we'd be back to reality in the morning, so it was very late by the time most people went to bed.

After my drinking session on Christmas Day, I'd volunteered for the late night guard shift to give other people the chance to enjoy themselves. (I was also feeling guilty about the evenings I'd spent at the base enjoying myself in the pub). Making sure that Stanley and Daisy, who by now were both exhausted, were tucked up in bed, I joined Paul, who had also volunteered for the late shift on the barricades.

Having not slept for over twenty-four hours, it took a lot of coffee to keep me awake.

We sat in the sentry box, listening to the revelry behind us and sheltering from the biting wind and the snow that had begun to fall steadily. Paul told me that until the soldiers who were due to be relieved had returned to base with the return convoy, he planned to take advantage of the extra manpower he had available and attack the farmhouse where we knew the people who had ambushed us were based.

The plan hadn't changed from the one I'd been told about previously. The following night Paul would surround the farmhouse with a strong force of men and vehicles. Just before daybreak, a UAV would launch a few missiles to destroy the building. If necessary, he would follow these up with a volley of AT4 anti-bunker shoulder-launched missiles, before sending in the troops to clear up.

It was a simple plan, and with the technology and weaponry we had at our disposal, it should pose the least risk to his soldiers.

After finishing my guard duty I collapsed, exhausted, into bed and didn't wake up until around midday.

CHAPTER TWENTY TWO

The following day started late for most of the community, as hangovers were being nursed. About six inches of snow lay on the ground and it was still falling steadily. The tracks left by the other groups, as they slowly made their way home after a hearty breakfast, soon disappeared.

Most of the soldiers were busy preparing for the attack on the farmhouse, and Pete, realising that some members of the community were suffering from a general lack of enthusiasm, gave up and declared a day of rest. The adults mostly sat around the fires at home and chatted, while the children made snowmen and engaged in snowball fights.

During the afternoon, I sought out Paul and asked if he would need any help from the community in the upcoming attack. He said he didn't need any help with the actual mission, but if we could take over some of the sentry duties, it would free up more soldiers to take part in the attack.

I spoke to Pete, and he willingly set about re-working the rotas and rounding up more volunteer sentries.

Paul was happy that it was snowing, because it would help to muffle any sounds they made on their approach. The UAV would still be able to fly and release its missiles, so he considered the weather to be an advantage. I hadn't been present when the soldiers were preparing for the Gumin attack, and was impressed by the care taken to check and re-check every single piece of equipment they were taking.

Allan had inspected the weapons we'd been given and had spent the day in the front room of Pete's house, learning how to strip and clean both the SA80 and the Light Machine Gun, disassembling them and putting them back together. Michelle had teased him about having a new love in his life.

He kept insisting that it was necessary, so that he could familiarise himself with the weapons, and only stopped when Pete and I joked that we wouldn't be surprised to see him running up and down the road, holding one of the guns and making pretend machine gun noises, just as Stanley did whenever he found a gun-shaped stick in the garden.

The civilian visitors were generally settling in well. Most of them had mixed with the rest of us from the outset, and had clearly enjoyed themselves at the previous night's celebration. Like the rest of us, they were making the most of the day of rest. Some of them were using the time to visit and introduce themselves to the people on the road they had yet to meet. I did notice that three of them weren't quite as sociable as the others. They were friendly enough, but so far, they'd kept to themselves and spent most of their time huddled together in the kitchen area, talking.

I didn't give it much thought. They were our guests, but they weren't really our responsibility. We were happy enough to show them what we'd done in order to survive. Hopefully, they would learn from this and pass on their knowledge when the time came for them to help existing communities or form new ones.

We didn't need to make friends with them. It was helpful if they were friendly, and in the short time that they were with us, made the effort to get along with the community, as they would probably get more out of their experience by doing so. If they chose not to be, that was their choice.

I reasoned to myself that I was probably being a bit unfair. They'd only arrived the day before and had been thrown straight into work and then the New Year's Eve party. They probably just needed some time to settle in. I decided I'd make the effort to chat to them later, as I understood that Pete had included all the new arrivals in the revised guard duty rota to help cover for the soldiers Paul was taking on the raid.

The snow continued to fall steadily, and by the time it was dark, there was at least twelve inches on the ground. Paul informed us that they were ready to depart, and that once the soldiers had eaten a hot meal and taken a short rest, they would make their way to the farm and get into their positions before daybreak. He was confident that the mission would be a complete success and that the occupants of the farmhouse were unlikely to survive the initial missile strike. If they did, they were unlikely to be in any fit state to offer resistance when the ground troops went in. He had some reservations about leaving us with only a few soldiers, but he was sure that we were more than capable of defending ourselves. In the meantime, he would be up against an unknown enemy with modern weapons. He needed plenty of men on the ground, as well as technological superiority, to guarantee their success.

We all urged him not to worry. He was, after all, going to deal with what we believed to be our closest threat.

Harry was staying behind with a small contingent of soldiers and he was cheerfully organising them to fit in with Pete's revised sentry rota. I hadn't witnessed it the previous night, as I'd been on guard duty, but apparently Harry and Kim, the young girl who had been rescued from St Agnes Road, had been getting along very well and had spent a good deal of the time chatting quietly in a corner. Perhaps it was the lack of television or other distractions, but the community had lost no time in speculating about "the romance of the century" and a possible future royal wedding. Harry seemed amused, but didn't deny anything, so perhaps the gossips were onto something. I visualised the future press interviews:

"So Kim, what first attracted you to the multi-millionaire prince of the realm?"

The road looked beautiful covered in its blanket of snow. The soft glow of the lights was diffused and reflected back, and any noise was quickly deadened by the softness of the surroundings.

Pete had issued more coal to each household in an effort to ward of the cold, and the smell of burning coal further enhanced the sense of tranquillity and security.

The peace was shattered briefly by the sound of engines revving and vehicles starting up. The soldiers boarded the fleet of vehicles and left to begin their mission. The falling snow quickly muffled the sound of the engines and silence fell again. The sentries huddled into their jackets and counted off the minutes until they could come off duty.

Becky was down for guard duty from ten until midnight and I gave her a hug as she left. I told her she looked very sexy, wrapped up in her thickest coat, with a scarf wrapped tightly around her neck and wearing her ski hat with her skiing goggles perched on her head. The look was finished off with a shotgun slung over her shoulder.

"You're every man's dream," I teased. "Warm and dangerous!" She pulled a face at me and set off through the snow.

Once the children were asleep and I'd spent some time with Jane and Michael, I climbed into bed to get some sleep before my next guard shift.

The sound of shotguns and an automatic weapon firing woke me up with a jolt. Shaking off the sleep, I reached out for Becky. She wasn't there. Grabbing the torch that was kept by the bed, I switched it on. Her side of the bed hadn't been slept in, and the clock on the bedside table showed that it was 11:45. She was still on guard duty and we were under attack!

Grabbing what clothes I could find and throwing them on, I hurried down the stairs, shoved my feet into a pair of boots, snatched up my MP5 and ran out of the door. More shots could be heard from the top of the road.

"Oh Christ, that's where Becky is!" I thought, as I pushed my way through the snow. I could see other people running out of doors, weapons in hand. We'd practised this over and over and I had to trust that the others would follow the procedures we'd established.

In the event of an attack, at any time, anyone not involved in defence had to make their way to my house and lock it down. I'd left my children in bed, possibly still asleep, but I had to make sure that Becky was OK. All the children had been well trained and drilled in the routine as well, so they knew what to expect and what to do.

Just in front of the barricade was a body lying in the snow. It was face down and the snow beneath it was dark with blood. It was wrapped in a large coat and it wasn't possible to tell who it was.

"Becky!" I screamed.

Throwing myself down next to the body, I turned it over. It wasn't Becky. Relief washed over me, swiftly followed by horror. It was Dave. From the gash on his neck, it looked as if his throat had been cut.

Dave and his wife Jo were enthusiastic and helpful members of our community from the beginning. Their children, Billy and Katie, were about the same age as Stanley and Daisy and were good friends.

But he was on the safe side of the barricade. Who had done this?

My thoughts were racing. Where was Becky? Holding my gun ready, I jumped up on to the barricade. A soldier was sprawled across it, face up. He'd been shot numerous times in the chest. More residents were arriving and everyone was demanding to know what had happened.

At some point in the night it had stopped snowing and the clouds had lifted. The light of the moon reflected off the snow and the entire scene was bathed in an eerie half-light. Further up the road I could see movement. More shots rang out. Without thinking, I jumped over the barricade and ran through the open gates, towards where the army vehicles were parked, ploughing through the knee deep snow as fast as I could.

I could see a soldier, holding a rifle out in front of him, dragging another soldier by his webbing. He was trying to make for cover as bullets hit the snow around him.

Taking a chance that he must be one of our men as he was being shot at, I slid to a stop behind the wall he was trying to reach. I got his attention by shouting at him, and grabbing him by his coat, I pulled him backwards and helped him get his friend behind cover. The injured soldier had been shot in the leg, and was conscious but in a lot of pain.

"What happened?" I shouted at him.

"I don't know. We'd just finished our guard shift and we were getting my kit bag out from one of the lorries. As we were walking back we heard shots from the barricade. We ran forward to investigate, came under fire and Jimmy got hit. There were three blokes, and they all had guns."

"Why didn't you shoot back?" I asked, exasperated.

My heart stopped when he said, "They had three women with them. I couldn't get a clear shot. They were struggling, but they were dragging them along."

"Which women?" I demanded, frantically.

"I don't know. I only got here yesterday. One was that woman Prince Harry was chatting up last night, I think the other one was the girlfriend of that copper. The last one I do know, I talked to her last night. Her name's Becky. When we walked up to get my kit bag, I noticed all three of them were sitting in the shelter on the barricade, talking."

"Who were the three men?" I asked. His answer shocked me.

"They came from the base. They were always hanging out together back then. They never mixed much with the rest of us."

I looked over the wall I was shcltcring behind. About fifty metres away I spotted two of the men pushing Becky into the back of the only armoured vehicle still parked there. The rest of the vehicles, apart from a few lorries, had all gone on the mission.

She was fighting them as hard as she could. I couldn't see Michelle or Kim. They must already have been in the vehicle. One of the men punched Becky in the face to stop her attacking him.

She collapsed in the snow, he picked her up and threw her into the back of the vehicle.

Seeing this, cold fury overtook me. I leapt over the wall and started to make my way towards them. I was going to rip their heads off with my bare hands. As one of the men stepped into the open I raised my weapon and opened fire, trying to hit him as I struggled through the knee-deep snow.

My gun clicked empty and I saw him raise his weapon.

The world slowed down.

He was aiming straight at me, there was a flash from his muzzle, followed by searing pain and then darkness …

ABOUT THE AUTHOR

Chris Harris was born in South Birmingham in 1971. Apart from a few years in his early twenties, he has spent his whole life in the city, he is truly a born and bred "Brummie", and rightly proud of this fact.

He settled on Moseley as his postcode of choice about fifteen years ago, and has become absorbed and entwined into the strong community found there.

He is a loyal and active member of Chantry Tennis Club, where he demonstrates his talents on (and off) the court.

He is also a loyal supporter of the several local music festivals and a number of local charities. He champions supporting the local independent economy, and so is a regular at the many local independent pubs and restaurants Moseley is rightly famous for.

His early career centered around the building trade, moving onto property development. Now Chris is a family man with a wife and three children, all of whom are very important to him and keep him very busy. His many interests include: tennis, skiing, racquet ball, darts, shooting and he has always been an avid reader.

He came late to writing, but it has really ignited something long buried within him. It has given him an outlet for his imagination, and never one to be short of an opinion or the last word, has enjoyed "putting it down on paper" in his books.

He reports that the UK Dark series "will be at least a trilogy, but you never know what's going to happen until you start writing" and is also trying his hand at a Zombie book.

Follow him on Facebook at Chris Harris Author

AUTHORS NOTE

Who would have thought that a year ago I would be writing a note at the end of my second book?

Not me for a start.

The writing started as more of a whim. An, "I wonder if I can do that" thought. Then one day I decided to have a go at.

It would not have been possible to even get half way through the first book, let alone even consider a second one, without the help and support of my wonderful wife Nicky. She made it happen by letting me off jobs that needed doing around the house, listening and putting up with my endless talking about my progress, and when I proudly showed her my first effort that I thought was brilliant, she gently reminded me that commas and paragraphs were possibly a good idea to include in the next draft. Thank you.

Billy and Katie, aka Stanley and Daisy. You are as brilliant as the characters in the book are. Don't stop being you!

Thanks to my many friends, old and new ones I have made through writing these books. Your support and putting up with me boring you to death constantly is really appreciated. (I have started to recognise the signs of eyes glazing over now.)

If you are mentioned in the book, you know who you are and remember, you chose your character.

Thanks to my volunteer beta readers. Shawn Graveling, Chris Garland of Forest Skills Ltd, Simon Wood, Janet Forshaw and Paul "Petal" Berry (recognise any names?). Your efforts and honest feedback have an incalculable value. Don't panic if your character has not appeared yet, there is still time!

Thank you for taking the time to read it. If you like it, please leave a review. If you didn't enjoy it, then you have my apologies for getting as far as these few words, and please feel free to contact me via Facebook on how it could have been better.

Please follow me on Facebook for news and updates.

Thank you for reading.

Chris Harris

Printed in Great Britain
by Amazon

65251353R00220